Death Stretch

by

Ashantay Peters

Death Stretch

Cover Art by *Diana Carlile*

The Wild Rose Press, Inc.
PO Box 708
Adams Basin, NY 14410-0708
Visit us at www.thewildrosepress.com

Publishing History
First Crimson Rose Edition, 2013
Digital ISBN 978-1-61217-961-2
Print ISBN 978-1-62830-148-9

Published in the United States of America

I watched Detective Johnson inhale, like he held in a rant. Shame on me, but pissing off the man held a certain appeal.

He took a breath through his nose, his gaze lifted for divine inspiration, or perhaps patience. "Break-ins are common these days, so maybe you should use the dead bolt."

"How do you know I don't?"

"The lock didn't tumble before you opened your door."

"Oh." It's hard to be sarcastic to a guy whose job is to "protect and serve." Speaking of serve, those lips could offer... no, I wouldn't go there.

"So, Detective Johnson, what *does* bring you by?"

"I have a few more questions. Mind if I come in?"

My brain stopped at the word *come*. Silly, but have I mentioned it's been awhile since I've dated?

He grabbed my arm. "Ms. Sheridan? Katie?"

The sizzle of his touch jolted me back to life. "Um, sure. Sorry, I haven't cleaned yet today." Or last week, but who's keeping count? And why apologize?

I closed the woman's magazine I'd left open to an article on *Giving Good Head* and shoved it under a pile of papers, hoping Detective Johnson hadn't noticed my reading preference. His smirk suggested he probably had.

My attention shifted into hostess mode. I might be a slut wanna-be, but my Mama raised me right.

"Something to drink? I have iced tea, bottled water, Pepsi." I stopped before adding "wine and beer."

The smirk disappeared, and his jaw tightened. "All I want are answers."

Praise for *DEATH STRETCH*

"Ms. Peters does what we've all wanted to do—she kills off that snooty yoga instructor who's far too flexible. The author successfully combines laugh-out-loud humor with sweat-inducing suspense and delivers one of the best debut novels you'll ever read."

~*Robin Weaver, author of BLUE RIDGE FEAR*

"Suspense and romance seasoned with a lusty sense of humor—*DEATH STRETCH* is a fast, fun, laugh-laced read!"

~*Linda Lovely, author*

Dedication

Thanks to Robin Weaver—
she pushes me when I drag my heels
and is directly responsible for this book's existence.
And to Linda Lovely,
plot hole finder and line editor extraordinary.
In addition, both are excellent writers
and author role models.
Thanks, ladies!

Chapter One

A blackmailer had targeted my best friend. Otherwise, I'd be home in bed. Alone, but it'd still be better than sharing a warm yoga classroom with a bunch of bogus corpses.

Sweat rolled off my forehead, trickled to my jaw, and flowed to the pool of moisture between my boobs. We'd been instructed to keep our eyes closed, but my impatience trumped the yoga master's directive. I peeped at my limber classmates. If the pile of bodies really were dead, the studio would stink. The room didn't smell all that great anyway.

The elevator music that had pushed me closer and closer to a coma-like state since the class began stalled, hiccupped, and resumed. Still, no one moved. Including me.

I rolled my head toward my friend's pretzel-twisted leg. "Ginger." My whisper reverberated through the room, louder than intended. Huh. No surprise there.

"Katie, shh. We're supposed to lie quietly." Her lips hadn't moved.

Ginger's clear yet almost inaudible speaking tone chastised me, and I lowered my voice. "When can we get up? I gotta pee."

My friend didn't blink. Truly, she's a guru. "Any minute now. Morgan should end the session soon."

I enrolled in the Saturday morning yoga class with

Ginger to find the creep that threatened her. Someone was blackmailing Ginger, and she suspected a class member, or even the instructor. I'd joined the class to help her discover the villain, but I wasn't sure why she thought I could help. Reading mysteries non-stop isn't the same as solving them.

The instructor, Morgan Anderson, personified hunk. Not my type, but eye candy is, well, eye candy. His hunk-squared muscles were hard to ignore. Ginger and I didn't want to believe anyone that pretty could be the blackmailer, but wouldn't rule anyone out.

Relaxing into the corpse pose didn't happen. I rolled to the side, sat up, and waited out my dizzy attack. "I need to pee, and I'm thirsty."

"Go already." Ginger's whisper provided all the encouragement I needed.

I stood. Crap. Classroom courtesy demanded I pick up my mat before leaving the studio, but if I bent over, I'd wet my yoga pants.

Oh hell. I'd come back for my stuff. Everyone was sure to leave the room in a few minutes anyway.

I picked my way through the sea of mats and yoga outfits, probably all organic cotton except for mine. Morgan's well-packaged muscles blocked my path to the bathroom. I stopped two feet from the instructor and crossed my legs, jiggling in place to keep myself—and the floor—dry. His chiseled lips looked ready to open and twist into a semblance of my most-disliked grade school teacher's sneer.

His expression didn't change, but I wasn't fooled. Mrs. Crankshaw, the afore-mentioned teacher, looked the same way right before she slapped me with detention. Every time I needed the bathroom.

A fly circled Morgan's nose, looking for a place to land. He didn't flinch. Although his composure made me wonder, I had to move. He wouldn't lie still much longer and I *really* had to go. *Go* being the operative word.

I looked over my shoulder as I entered the bathroom. Everyone was as still as death. I hoped no one could hear me doing my business. Leaving the studio early was embarrassing enough.

Bladder empty, I crept back into the practice room, keeping to the edges to avoid Morgan. What the heck? Everyone still held the corpse pose. Something wasn't right. Skulking my way back to my friend, I stood above her, hands on hips.

"This doesn't feel right."

"You're right." Ginger sat up with a fluid motion, her red hair tumbling around her shoulders. That move from anyone else would spike my jealousy, but Ginger and I are best buds.

"Morgan?" Ginger's voice was as fluid as her sit-ups.

When he didn't answer, my friend headed toward him, I followed. We stopped several feet away, and for good reason. Mr. Hunk had vomit running down his chin, forming a small pool on his chest.

Even so, the dude didn't move. My gut rolled. The only psychic ability I have is located there, and I trust it. My innards screamed something was seriously wrong.

Ginger grabbed the towel lying at his feet and wiped his mouth clean. "Morgan?" The whisper disappeared. My friend sounded on the verge of hysteria. "Are you okay?"

Nothing. Nada. Zip. That wasn't good.

"What's going on?"

I twisted, almost bumping into the flashy blonde who'd sniffed when I first entered the studio. A quick glance showed most of our classmates hovered behind Flash, a.k.a. Blondie.

I grabbed Ginger's arm as she reached to touch Morgan. "Let me." I swallowed, trying not to inhale. Laying two fingers against a pulse point, I was afraid I'd find nothing and was almost right. "Holy crap. Somebody better call 9-1-1. Now."

"Katie, what's wrong?" Ginger's voice shook nearly almost as much as my fingers when I snatched them away from Morgan's neck. Her green eyes flashed in her pale face.

"His pulse is almost non-existent." I raised my voice. "We need a doctor. Fast. Has anyone called?"

My tone hit vibrato and cracked.

Ginger threw her arm around my shoulders. "Take it easy." Her presence comforted me, but my blood pressure surged, adrenaline shook my body.

The women moved forward, magnetically pulled in to the drama.

"Okay, everyone. Back away." Ginger took control, seeming to have shifted from panicked to person-in-charge in mere seconds. "Give Morgan room to breathe. While we're at it, let's all do some deep cleansing breaths." She pinched my arm.

I checked Morgan's pulse, just in case I'd made a mistake. Nope, I hadn't. While my fingers touched his neck, his pulse stuttered to a stop. I pulled my sweaty towel from around my neck. Throwing it over his chest, I jumped into continuous chest compressions. Excited chatter drove my adrenaline higher. Good thing I'd learned the new CPR technique at my construction company job. No way I wanted to put my lips on someone who'd collapsed the way he had, not even Hunky Morgan. My flat-handed rhythm didn't cease until the paramedics arrived and took over.

Too bad none of our efforts made a difference. A paramedic pronounced Morgan dead.

Who knew yoga could kill you?

****

Justin Nash, Morgan's assistant, ran into the room. "What's wrong?"

Silence dropped over the studio faster than the Times Square ball dropped on New Year's Eve.

Justin looked around. "Where's Morgan?"

The women standing around the instructor—or rather, former instructor—stepped aside. One of the paramedics had covered the large body with a blanket.

"Morgan?"

Justin saw us trying not to look at the instructor's body. He hurried to Morgan and dropped to his knees. Jerking back the blanket, he pushed on Morgan's shoulder. "What's wrong with him?"

I leaned forward to whisper, "Um, Justin? I'm sorry, but he's dead."

The paramedic frowned at me, momentarily marring a face I was sure matched Mr. January on my Rescue Hunks calendar.

"No, no, that can't be." Justin placed his palms against his cheeks. "Not Morgan. He's too young."

He dropped his head into his hands and sobbed. Ginger patted him on the small of his back.

No one said a word as a second paramedic re-entered the room, tucking a cell phone into his pocket. "The police want all of you to wait in the other room."

Police? Other room?

"Why?" Flash asked the question the rest of us were afraid to voice. I suppose when you're blonde, boob-enhanced, and beautiful, you can demand answers.

"Can't say." Mr. January appeared blonde-proof. "Please, everyone, move into the outer room."

We shuffled into the small office where all students left their shoes. Like the dozen or so shell-shocked classmates around me, I didn't look anyone else in the eye. Following a few minutes that felt like hours, sirens echoed off the downtown buildings then stopped, abrupt and final, outside the yoga studio.

"The cops are here." After stating the obvious, Flash leaned against one of the two windows in the second-floor space. "And that is one hot guy getting out of the unmarked car." She fanned herself in the time-honored gesture known to women across the planet.

I sat hunched into myself, Ginger at my side. We were the only two who hadn't charged forward to check out the scenery. Police. I'd been on the wrong side of the cops once too often in the past. They're not my favorite people.

Besides. Gawking over some hot cop seemed disrespectful to Morgan.

"Why are they here? It was food poisoning or a heart attack, wasn't it?" I hadn't meant to ask that out loud.

Ginger didn't answer but gripped my hand.

Flash turned from the window. "What makes you think some bad food affected his heart? Morgan's a stud, through and through. His stamina—" She broke off, conscious the group listened. "He could hold the downward facing dog pose longer than any yoga instructor I've worked with."

The exchanged smirks flying around the room implied everyone knew something I didn't, but I couldn't find the energy to care. I'd just performed CPR on a dead man. "Maybe it wasn't a heart attack, but he just died. Who called the police?"

A deep voice answered from the doorway. "I can answer that."

Heads turned in unison and we inhaled a roomful of oxygen in a collective breath. A deep, deep yoga breath. Flash hadn't exaggerated. A dark-haired man commanded the doorway, making an off-the-rack suit look designed only for him and sewn with loving hands.

"The paramedics are required to call us if the cause of death is questionable. I'm Detective Johnson, and my partner is Detective Pulaski. We'll be asking a few questions." His take-charge attitude attracted me as much as his six-foot-plus height, wide shoulders, and well-defined jaw. I even found his crooked nose and butchered haircut appealing.

Oh, Papa. Take me. Anywhere. I'll go quietly.

"You can start with me, Detective," Flash purred. "I've got nothing to hide."

My gaze appraised her runway-model figure in a molded, backless outfit. She wasn't lying.

****

"I'll need your name and address, miss." Pulaski was no slacker in the looks department either. A dimpled grin, not currently directed at me, and a flat stomach were just the appetizers. I'd had plenty of time to take inventory while waiting in the outer room. After over an hour, I'd finally been called into Morgan's office. Or I should say Morgan's former office. Grammar wasn't my strong suit.

I glanced at Cop Sexy Johnson, who'd planted his tall, dark and dangerous self on the desk. My mouth went a little dry, and not from the stress of being questioned by the police. Okay, so I'm a cliché.

Wrestling my demanding hormones under control, I cleared my throat. "So Morgan didn't die from food poisoning?"

Cop Sexy's stern expression chilled me. "We'll ask the questions."

"Okay." A pesky frog made my voice husky.

Sexy's stare put me in the deep freeze. Damn, a jacket would've been nice.

"We've been informed, Ms. Sheridan, that you left the room before the session ended."

The room's chill deepened to Antarctica level. "Yes, I had to, uh, use the bathroom."

He consulted his notes. "And you paused next to the deceased, is that correct?"

That sounded scary. Like I was a suspect. "Yup...yes that's correct."

"Did you touch Mr. Anderson at any time?"

"No."

"So you paused, walked past him and left the room. Is that right?" Disbelief colored his tone.

Cop Sexy no more. Nope, he'd turned to the dark side and had become Cop A-hole.

"That's right." I bit off my reply. Didn't care how it sounded.

"You're sure?"

His arrogance made my teeth hurt.

"Yes, I'm sure I know what I did." My anger finally broke through. "I had to pee, okay? And I thought Morgan would make me go back to my mat. Just like Mrs. Crankshaw sent me back to my desk." Crap. That wasn't supposed to come out.

"Mrs. Crankshaw?" He checked his notes. "She's not listed as a class member."

He waited.

I capitulated. "She was one of my grade school teachers." I'd hoped he'd let it go, but his raised eyebrow indicated I wouldn't get away without spilling all the sordid details. "She gave me detention or extra homework when I left class early. Mrs. Crankshaw never believed me when I said I had to go to the bathroom."

Detective Johnson's lips curved up at the corners. The sight was so pretty I forgot the highway and followed the turn. The curve dead-ended when his lips straightened. Johnson didn't comment, just sat with an air of expectation.

"One time she didn't believe me, but I really had to go and well, let's just say things got messy. The same thing would've happened today."

"Hmmm." His lips quirked. The creep. His throat clearing sounded like laughter. "Okay. Moving on. Did you know Mr. Anderson outside class?"

"What? No. I told you, I just started class today. I didn't know anyone. Except Ginger."

"Why did you enroll in Mr. Anderson's class?"

I almost blurted out "his muscles," but stopped myself in time. "My friend, Ginger." Her and a blackmailing jerk. "She thought I'd enjoy something new."

"That would be Ginger Howe?"

"That's right."

He looked at his notes again, but the gesture was a ruse. This guy knew where he was going and what he wanted.

"Ms. Sheridan, may I call you Kathryn?"

"Katie." I wondered if he thought that *Columbo* trick would work.

"With your hair, I'd have guessed Kat." He cleared his throat again. The man should have his sinuses checked.

My eyes narrowed. Wait. My hair? What did he mean? No way my long wavy hair looked like a cat's. Especially when a bad case of yoga mat head had every strand snarled like a web spun by a crack-crazed spider.

He blew out a breath. "You performed CPR?"

My pique dissipated. I recalled Morgan's pulse slowing, coming to a stop under my fingers. "Yes." My answer sounded quiet, even to my ears. "Yes."

"Did you notice any excessive sweat? Contorted features?"

He died. That seemed pretty damn unusual to me. "No, nothing."

Detective Johnson reached into his pocket and pulled out a business card. I took it with numb fingers and gave it a cursory glance.

I looked again and snorted. "Dirk? Your first name is Dirk?"

He shifted in his seat. "My mother named me after an actor."

I'd grown up watching old movies. "Really? Dirk Bogarde?"

He ran a finger around his collar. "Yeah."

I tilted my head, trying to remember some of Bogarde's roles but failed. "Didn't he play bad guys for a while?"

His eyes narrowed into slits. "I wouldn't know."

After gulping, I managed a reply. "Never mind."

He opened his mouth and I'm sure he was about to give me the standard warning so I blurted, "I know. Don't leave town."

He smiled and nodded. "We'll be in touch."

Whoa, baby. His low voice touched a nerve and Cop A-hole made a one-eighty back to Cop Sexy. Given my proximity to a murder, that wasn't a good thing.

Chapter Two

Chocolate. The only thing that could save the day was a cocoa-based gift from heaven. The Chocolate Fix on Main Street was closer and just as divine. Ginger and I headed there so fast, I almost ran. Even if nothing else about today scared me, two bouts of exercise in one six-hour stretch promised nightmares.

Most people would search for health and life after confronting death. Not me. Exercise or chocolate? Please. No contest.

I inhaled the unique aroma of the store, feeling my blood pressure drop with every breath. Jimmy Buffett has his frozen concoction that helps him hang on. I have chocolate. Less fuss, less muss, no frozen sinuses.

We bought truffles and settled into wrought iron chairs at the small marble-topped ice cream tables in front of the Fix's large front window. Sunshine flooded the dark ceramic floor tiles next to us, radiating welcome warmth. Even though spring bloomed outside, my bones ached from delayed shock.

Mona promised the hot chocolate we ordered would only take a minute but that sixty seconds sounded like a long wait. If you've ever been present when someone died, you know how I felt. Shaken, not stirred.

Ginger placed her hand over mine. "You okay?"

Nodding, I bit into a truffle dusted with cayenne.

The creamy ganache melted in my mouth while the spice reminded me I still lived and was glad of it.

My friend glanced at the chocolates beautifully displayed on a square white plate but didn't touch a single one. "This wasn't supposed to happen. I never thought you'd get caught up in my mess. It should have been simple. Find the blackmailer and report him to the cops before anyone found out."

By "anyone" she meant her husband, Rob. By my count, he didn't deserve her discretion.

"Ginger, you've saved my butt more often than I can remember. I'll have your back whenever you need help. Stop worrying and eat a truffle before I eat yours too."

She didn't move, not a millimeter, and her stillness scared me. God, gruff humor hadn't worked to make her feel better. Time to up the ante.

I placed my hand over hers and squeezed. "Ginger, we're the Demonic Duo." I waited. The corners of her lips twitched but she remained quiet. "Don't make me say it."

Ginger's lips curved up. "Say it."

"I really hate it when you make me go girly."

"Say it or I'll never share chocolate with you again." Despite her almost smile, tears welled in her brown eyes.

Oh, crap.

Grasping her hand, I took a deep breath and spoke past my dry throat. Declaring love out loud was not easy for me. I'd rather show it and Ginger knew that.

"I love you, Ginger. Don't do this, please."

Mona, the owner of Chocolate Fix, plopped two mugs of hot chocolate in front of us. "Don't do what?"

The hot drink, made with half-and-half, shaved Belgian chocolate and topped with real whipped cream, called to me like a siren to sailors. Not too sweet, smooth and silky, the rich confection had me ready to beach myself on the nearest rocky shore. I licked off my cream mustache before answering. "Get upset about what happened at the Yoga Studio."

Mona slid her generous curves onto a nearby chair and picked up the truffle Ginger and I planned to split. She noticed my raised eyebrow and shrugged. "I'll give you another one. Now, tell me, were you there when Morgan died?"

Ginger's mouth dropped open. "You know what happened already?"

"Your other classmates came in after the cops took their statements. What took you so long? I had to hear the news from some snarky blonde." Not waiting for an answer, she turned her attention to me. "I heard you tried to save him."

A nod seemed a good enough answer.

"Too bad. If I'd been there, I'd have told you not to bother."

A jolt ran through me, my spine straightened. This was a Mona I'd never seen before. Her eyes held fire, her cheeks stained a mottled pink and her breathing heavy. What the...?

Mona leaned closer. "The man was trouble." Her voice dropped. "His beauty was only skin deep, if you know what I mean."

Even though Mona was a long-time friend, this was Ginger's story. Her quickie affair with Morgan wouldn't just destroy her marriage. It could also land her in jail.

14

I caught Ginger's shadowed expression and stalled. "I'd never met Morgan before today. I'd seen him around, but that's it."

Mona sniffed. "You didn't miss much. Not unless you wanted to get screwed. The talk around town made him a maestro in bed."

Her face turned candy apple red. Huh? Maybe she was one of Morgan's multitudes.

Nah, I was pretty sure Mona didn't like men enough to exchange saliva with one. The blush must've come from the odd sense of decorum I'd noticed before. Odd because Mona had founded an original Hippie commune out west before moving to our little North Carolina town ten years ago.

I realized I didn't know much about Mona other than her incredible talent with chocolate, a skill that conferred sainthood on a person in my opinion. But, death, possibly murder, had a way of making you think twice about friends. Just what was her relationship with Morgan and why was she in such a snit?

Without glancing at Ginger, I responded. "No, I didn't know."

"He went from one woman to another like a chocoholic running through a five-pound box of Belgian truffles. Rumor had it, his studio was nothing more than a way to pull in harem candidates."

I'd bet my last bite of truffle that Mona referred to Flash. "Did the snarky blonde gossiping about Morgan's death in here look like a runway model?"

Mona nodded.

"She told everyone at the studio that Morgan was a stud."

"No doubt. But from the gossip today, he'd been

asking to be killed for months."

The store chimes rang and Mona moved to help a new customer. Ginger's face made a ghost look robust. I pushed the plate of truffles toward her and she lifted one to her mouth. It was easy to see she ate on autopilot.

"So what? You got hooked up with Svengali. Everyone makes mistakes. Sounds like you had company."

My friend smiled halfheartedly. "Yeah. That makes me feel better."

We finished our serotonin/sugar input in silence. The store grew crowded, and almost everyone discussed Morgan's death. Without speaking, Ginger and I got up and left. On the way out, I called to Mona. "We'll catch up with you later to redeem our extra truffle."

That's a promise we'd keep. Besides, I needed an excuse to talk with Mona with no one around. If she really had the skinny on Morgan, her info might help me identify Ginger's blackmailer.

"I didn't do it." Ginger's words sounded torn from her gut.

"I know. Goes without saying."

What neither of us wanted to discuss was who, in our small-town-turned-trendy-growth-suburb, might have murdered Morgan. Because his death sure hadn't looked natural.

Now that was a mystery I was happy I didn't have to solve.

****

The doorbell rang. What the...? My friends know to give a shout out and come on in. It's not like they'd be interrupting me doing the dirty with anyone. I haven't had a man in a while. Mona would say "way too long without sex," but I'm not Mona.

I grasped the doorknob, ready to throw open the door, when I realized I should probably check the peephole first. After a quick look, my hand flew off the knob. The long-lashed hazel eyes I'd peeped seemed a travesty in Detective Johnson's stern face.

My face warmed, and my pulse quickened. This was not good on too many levels. I was stymied for a moment.

The doorbell rang again, the sound impatient. Or maybe I picked up the vibes from the man on the other side. Would he be Cop Sexy or Cop A-hole? Either way, I was in deep. Might as well get 'er done. I threw open the door.

"Don't you know you're supposed to ask who's at the door before you open it?"

Ah, my answer. Cop A-hole had arrived.

"Don't you know a peephole when you see one?"

"What, this thing?" His finger flicked dismissively toward my lighted Kokopelli flute-playing doorbell/peephole combination. One of my former boyfriends installed it before taking off for Arizona. The gizmo didn't fit in with my Southern small town, but sometimes neither did I.

"My peeper does the job. You came here to insult me, is that right?"

I watched him inhale, like he held in a rant. Shame on me, but pissing off the man held a certain appeal.

He took a breath through his nose, his gaze lifted for divine inspiration, or perhaps patience. "Break-ins are common these days, so maybe you should use the dead bolt."

"How do you know I don't?"

"The lock didn't tumble before you opened your door."

"Oh." It's hard to be sarcastic to a guy whose job is to "protect and serve." Speaking of serve, those lips could offer... no, I wouldn't go there.

"So, Detective Johnson, what *does* bring you by?"

"I have a few more questions. Mind if I come in?"

My brain stopped at the word *come*. Silly, but have I mentioned it's been awhile since I've dated?

He grabbed my arm. "Ms. Sheridan? Katie?"

The sizzle of his touch jolted me back to life. "Um, sure. Sorry, I haven't cleaned yet today." Or last week, but who's keeping count? And why apologize?

I closed the woman's magazine I'd left open to an article on *Giving Good Head* and shoved it under a pile of papers, hoping Detective Johnson hadn't noticed my reading preference. His smirk suggested he probably had.

My attention shifted into hostess mode. I might be a slut wanna-be, but my Mama raised me right.

"Something to drink? I have iced tea, bottled water, Pepsi." I stopped before adding "wine and beer."

The smirk disappeared and his jaw tightened. "All I want are answers."

His sudden mood change threw me. I struggled for composure. Cop A-hole had returned.

He consulted his notebook. "A witness reports you bent over and touched Anderson's body before you left the room. Care to tell me why your accounts differ?"

Oh, let me count the ways. "First, I told you—I didn't bend over or touch Morgan's body. I stopped to make sure he hadn't seen me then I scooted to the bathroom. Second, I don't know who told you something different, but I'd like to know why they lied. Third, if I had bent over, you would have seen the puddle, because I really had to pee."

Crap. I hadn't meant to say that last part aloud.

Detective Johnson looked away, but not before I saw his grin. He cleared his throat. "Maybe you should stop drinking from that big bottle of water you carry. No wonder you need the bathroom so often."

"Toxins. I flush them with water."

"Leading to the Mrs. Crankshaw effect."

We faced each other so I couldn't miss his raised eyebrow. "What?"

"Don't tell me you're on some weird diet. Having as many curves as the Blue Ridge Parkway isn't a bad thing." He coughed and looked at his notes.

My stomach dropped deliciously. I could fall in love with this version of the man. I squashed that thought under my steel-toed work boot. "Who said I bent over and touched the body? Everyone had their eyes closed."

"Apparently not everyone."

"I guess someone could have seen me standing. When I looked around, everyone seemed lost in Nirvana. The place you're supposed to find with meditation, not the band."

"So you looked around? Why? Feeling guilty? Or making sure there were no witnesses?"

"I didn't do anything to Morgan. I didn't even know the man." I stopped to control my temper but my raised voice proved my failure. "Who said I did more than stand there?"

He didn't answer my question. "If you were leaving the room, why didn't you take your things with you? Isn't that proper yoga etiquette?"

How did he know yoga etiquette? Finally I had a clue to my accuser's identity. The finger pointer had to be Flash. She'd made a big deal about my not removing my shoes instantly when I walked in the door. I knew I didn't like her. But why would she lie about my actions? And why had she been watching me? "I told you. It was my first lesson. I had to use the bathroom. I figured everyone would be up when I returned to the room."

"So your story is you didn't know the victim, didn't bend over him and didn't kill him. Is that right?"

"Right." My pulse slowed and my chest ached. "Was he really murdered?"

He ran a hand through his hair. "Yes, he really was murdered."

"Why?"

"I'm working to answer that question. Meanwhile, don't—"

"Yeah, I know. Don't leave town."

He grinned. "No, I was going to say don't forget to lock your door. Any nut job could get in here."

"Including you?" Dang, there went my smart mouth again.

He shook his head. "I don't want another case on my overloaded desk because you're too naïve to take precautions."

"So I'm off the suspect list?"

"I didn't say that. We're investigating everyone. I'll be back when I have more questions." "Don't forget to lock your door." He pointed his index finger at me.

"And don't leave town."

"Sheesh."

He stomped out the door, leaving me with too many questions and a vague sense of unrest. If only we hadn't gotten interrupted at Mona's before she'd told us why Morgan had been headed to Corpseville.

Crap. I should have mentioned Mona to Detective Johnson. On second thought, good thing I hadn't. Her information could lead the cops right back to Ginger.

Chapter Three

Ginger answered on the first ring, her voice low and urgent. "I can't talk now. Rob just got home. I'll call you later."

I stared at the receiver, the dial tone loud and clear. What the ...?

My stomach growled almost as loud as the dial tone, so I replaced the receiver and headed for the kitchen. Ginger never hung up on me. And where had her husband been on a Sunday morning? He wasn't a church-going man, and a small paunch indicated he'd taken a hiatus from running.

Morgan's death was making me crazy. Ginger and I considered Morgan an unlikely blackmailer. So the threat remained. Maybe Mona could shed light on the situation.

I hopped on my bike and headed for the Chocolate Fix. Yeah, I know. More exercise on the same weekend. I needed to stop before fitness turned into a habit, but I had no choice. My car sat in the shop and the bike remained my only transportation. Ginger offered to lend me a car but I didn't want the responsibility. The combined cost of the Howe vehicles could purchase three of my bungalows.

****

Dang. I stood in front of the Fix, lungs heaving and sweat once more pouring off my forehead. Too bad I forgot Mona closed on Sunday, but then it wasn't every weekend I became a murder suspect.

I should let things go. Yeah. Just go home.

Avoiding my sweaty reflection in the store window, I eased onto the bike seat and peddled toward home. I didn't need a mirror to know my black hair stuck to my head, and my brown eyes looked like they belonged on a velvet painting.

Having taken the same route hundreds of times, I pedaled by rote, barely noticing the houses of friends and neighbors I passed every day. Too bad I couldn't put my brain on automatic. My mind kept replaying the previous day's events. Detective Johnson stayed at the forefront of the memories.

Morgan's face floated to mind. Such a vital man. Dead.

Ginger, threatened by a blackmailer who might or might not have been Morgan.

Me, questioned by the police. Treated like a criminal. Told I couldn't leave town.

Could my life get any worse?

The hair on the back of my neck stood up. Glancing over my shoulder, I saw a dark SUV with tinted windows ten feet behind me. Strange. He had plenty of room to pass me on the back street. The engine noise revved up.

Time to get this moron on his way. I motioned for him to pass, but he hung back. The engine raced. I glanced over my shoulder. Sunlight glared off the SUV's chrome grill. I winced. My eyes closed, but not before I saw the vehicle veer toward me. Crap, he wouldn't miss me. I needed to move and fast.

I swerved to the side and ran up the Haywood's

driveway, steering with one hand. I hit a rock. The bike dropped to the side and so did I. My hands took the brunt of the impact, scraping as I sandpapered the cement. I rolled to a sitting position.

The SUV raced off, now too far away to catch the plate. If I hadn't turned sharply onto the drive, I'd be hamburger.

My hands stung. I cradled them to my chest, breathing quickly and trying not to cry. I don't know how long I'd been blubbering when Mrs. Haywood ran from her house, a first-aid kit in one hand and cell phone in the other. My mind blanked as she fussed over me.

I had to stop asking rhetorical questions. Yes, life could get worse. Much worse. If the SUV driver hadn't just proved that fact, the arriving car did. Detectives Johnson and Pulaski arrived on the scene.

"So you're working Traffic Division now?" I bit my bottom lip but the gesture didn't retract my words.

Dirk raised his eyebrows and looked to his partner. Detective Pulaski shrugged and answered. "Just lucky. We were the closest unit."

"We'd have stopped anyway. When a suspect or material witness is involved in any altercation, we get notified," Dirk said.

Mrs. Haywood gasped and spurted half a tube of antiseptic cream on my hands. She trembled and leaned away from me. "I'm sorry dear. I wouldn't have called the police if I'd known."

I looked her in the eyes. "Mrs. Haywood, Detective Johnson is teasing. You've known me for years. Do you really think I'm mixed up with criminals?"

She thought about my question a beat too long.

"Well, dear, I knew you and Ginger formed a club. What was it called again?" She placed a finger against her lips and tilted her head. "Oh, yes, the Dynamic Duo, wasn't it?" She chuckled. "You two did get into a fair amount of scrapes as I recall."

I closed my eyes against the harsh reality of former teachers and small town life.

Against admittedly low odds, a low male voice heightened my shame. "Dynamic Duo, huh? Which one of you was Batman and which one Robin?"

I didn't bother to correct his impression. Demonic Duo didn't have the same cache. His amusement vibrated the air but I ignored him. Well, tried to ignore him. The man had presence.

"You didn't need to stop. I fell off my bike. No big deal."

Detective Johnson narrowed his eyes at me. I narrowed mine back.

"The call was reported a hit and run."

"Who called it a hit and run?"

Mrs. Haywood placed her hand on my arm. "I did, dear, remember?"

I kept my tone airy. "Oh, you know SUV drivers. Either they think they own the road or they can't see over the dash. There was no *hit*. I had an accident."

"Was it a dark SUV?"

"I guess so. They all look alike, but I think it had a Cadillac insignia. Why?"

He put his hands on my shoulders and squeezed. Warmth exploded and shot down my spine.

"Morgan Anderson drove an Escalade. His assistant reported the keys missing."

"Why would... Huh?"

25

"I told you earlier. You need to be careful." He released my shoulders but watched me.

"I can take care of myself."

He snorted, somehow making his honk sound sexy. "Right."

"Yeah, right, I can."

He shook his head. "You're one hard-headed woman." He motioned to Pulaski. "Let's get the bike loaded."

"Hey, where do you think you're going with my bicycle?"

He pointed to the mangled frame and flat front tire. "You really think you can ride this?"

"No," I muttered.

"Sorry, I didn't hear you."

I raised my voice to just under a shout. "I said, no."

"We'll give you a ride home."

"I can walk. I've gotten scraped up before."

"Hey, Matt, you ever see such a stubborn woman?"

"Yeah, my mother, my sisters, my ex."

Dirk turned to me. "You're coming with us. No arguments."

Throughout my ordeal, Mrs. Haywood had stayed by my side. Her whisper caught my attention. "You should go after him, dear. He's quite handsome and sparks fly between you. I think it's Kismet."

With that, she got to her feet, picked up her phone and first-aid supplies and scurried home. Sparks fly, my ass.

I sprung up after her. Okay, the truth is I barely concealed my groans as I rose. My knees had escaped Mrs. Haywood's frenzied nursing, so they didn't sport bandages or oily antiseptic. Didn't make the scrapes hurt less. A sore right hip and a bruised keister added to the mix.

The two detectives loaded my battered bike into their trunk, me into their backseat and themselves into the front. We left the scene, my ego more bruised than my body. And my body was in rough shape.

My head spun. Could this day - no, I wouldn't ask.

****

We pulled into my drive and Johnson jumped out and ran to my porch. I might've been charmed with his actions but being locked in the backseat ticked me off. Royally. This "he who shall be obeyed" crap rubbed me raw.

Johnson stomped back to the car. Uh, oh, trouble. His red face and hunched shoulders clued me in. I inched to the middle of the seat, ignoring the shiny brown stain next to me. Matt Pulaski lowered the window as his partner walked up. "What's wrong?"

Johnson waved his large hand at me. "Her."

Uh, oh, not trouble. Deep shit.

"What did I tell you?"

I wondered if his eyes were loaded, because I sensed a heat-seeking missile. "About what and which time?"

I spotted Pulaski's grin in the rearview mirror. I suppressed my own and tried my innocent expression on Johnson.

"Didn't I tell you to lock your damn door?"

"I did." Did I? I couldn't remember and that disturbed me. "I'm pretty sure I did."

Pulaski was already out of the car. "You want to take a look."

Dirk nodded. Both detectives drew their guns and

headed for my home. *My home.*

My throat grew dry. My imagination hit overdrive. Why would anyone break in?

The scrapes on my hands vied with sandpaper-dry eyes, and a lump the size of a baby Komodo dragon formed in my throat. I kicked the back of the seat, forgetting the protective steel mesh, and added a sore foot to my list of injuries.

A week passed. Okay, about three minutes, but every second seemed like an hour. The cops finally exited my bungalow and holstered their guns. Pulaski nodded at Dirk and trotted to my closest neighbor's house. He wouldn't find anyone home, but I kept my mouth shut. My self-appointed hero placed his hand on the car roof and leaned down.

"Let me out of here." My voice sounded like a caged animal's.

"I'm thinking we should keep you in protective custody for your own good, sweetheart."

My lungs seized up, but held enough air for a little tantrum. "I'm not your sweetheart. Cripes sake, we just met." That out, I breathed free. "Besides, you said I'm a material witness, remember?"

I lost steam. "Not only that, I want to see my house. How bad is it?" My wimpy tone made me cringe, but the question was already out there.

"*Nichts.*" Pulaski's voice threw me because I hadn't seen him return.

Nicks? Huh?

"Nothing? You sure?" Dirk asked.

Pulaski nodded.

"Okay then." Dirk opened my door and extended his hand.

"I'm scraped, not helpless."

They exchanged grins. Dirk dropped his hand. "Habit. Most folks sitting in the back are handcuffed."

My face heated as I climbed out. I hurried toward the house, scrapes and bruises forgotten—then stopped at the threshold, uncertain. Pulling in a big breath, I pushed open the door. Behind me Cop Sexy's presence sent waves of heat up my spine.

Papers and magazines covered most surfaces. Haphazard piles of books topped the magazines. The incriminating "giving head" magazine article lay open on the couch. My gaze ran from the overflowing bookshelves to the dying hanging plants to the medium-thick dust layer covering the tables. My sweaty yoga clothes sat in a plastic grocery bag on the floor.

I exhaled. Nothing wrong. Well, nothing that some cleaning wouldn't fix.

"Couldn't tell for sure, but the place looks the same as it did earlier." His tone sounded amused. "Is anything out of place? Or missing?" I turned in time to see him eyeing the magazine—still open to the "head" article.

My back went up. "Hey, I like to read." I strode to the couch, closed the magazine and tossed it face down on the table.

"I see. You've been reading that same article for a while."

My fingers itched to snatch him bald. Bless his dark, trouble-making heart.

"Ms. Sheridan, would you please check the rest of your home while we're here?" Pulaski's voice of reason kicked me into gear.

Ignoring Dirk, I limped through the rest of my

bungalow. Nothing seemed out of place, but I felt uneasy. I couldn't put my finger on anything specific, but the suspicion someone had been inside my humble abode stuck with me.

"Are you okay?" Dirk reached for me but stopped just before touching my arm. The aborted gesture stayed between us.

"Yeah. I think so."

"Then we'll leave." He pulled out a card and Pulaski did the same. "Call one of us if anything happens."

I took their cards and stuck them in my pocket.

Dirk pointed to my pants. "Pull those cards out and put them by the phone."

"Yes, sir, Mr. Cop A—"

I shut my mouth. He grinned and followed with an unexpected, way too endearing wink. My heart raced and I watched two fine behinds walk to my door.

"And lock the damn door after us."

That did it. The fantasy died.

Chapter Four

My favorite investigative news show blared from the living room. I'm not a big fan of television, but that was one show I tried to catch every Sunday. I liked to see the bad guys sweat.

The onions I chopped gave my sinuses a workout, and I grabbed a tissue. The hair on my neck stood up. Someone watched me.

No. Someone was in the house.

I looked for a weapon. Nothing was close. Could I get to the knife on the chopping block? Could I even use force against another human? No doubt allowed. My bandaged hand reached for the blade.

"Ms. Sheridan."

Holy crap, it was Johnson. I crossed my legs to keep from wetting myself. Equal parts of relief and pique filled me. I didn't know whether to kiss him or cuss him out.

"I advised you to lock your door. What part of L-O-C-K translates to O-P-E-N in your brain?"

Cussing him won the argument. My hand wanted to keep moving for the knife. Since I didn't want jail time, I refrained. Still, relenting was a close decision.

"Detective Johnson, how nice of you to drop in. Uninvited. You're trespassing, aren't you?"

He leaned against the doorjamb looking better than he ought. "I have cause."

I lifted my eyebrow. Oh, all right, both brows went up. I still hadn't mastered the one eyebrow lift like Cop Sexy.

"No answer when I knocked, Ms. Sheridan. Television too loud. Known occupant present at the scene of a recent crime. Door unlocked. All signs of a problematic situation. I called out when I entered. You didn't answer."

"I didn't hear you."

"See, a crime could have been committed. I'm right to investigate."

My hand remained hovered above the knife. Cop Sexy noticed. Naturally, I dropped my arm to my side. "Why are you really here?"

The hot olive oil smell recalled me to my task. A loud sizzle greeted my addition of onion and garlic to the frying pan.

He scratched his cheek. "I forget."

My growl echoed louder than the hiss of cooking green peppers and fresh mushrooms. A rush of familiar aromas hit the air. I kept my head down, my hands busy stirring. Cop Sexy's grin was so big I could feel the heat from five feet away.

"Okay. I'll stop teasing. Mind if I sit down?"

He'd already pulled out a chair at my table, so I didn't bother answering. Reaching into a pocket, he removed his notebook and pen. "I have a few more questions."

My temper came out to play. "Look, I've had a bad weekend and I just want to eat dinner and relax. Can't we talk some other time?"

"Ms. Sheridan, Katie, look. My interview won't take long and you could provide some important insights."

"Yeah, right. Did *someone* tell you I did something else? Maybe kiss the corpse? Pull the other one." The skillet required my attention. Time for fresh tomatoes.

"Huh? Pull the other what?"

"Pull the other leg. We both know there's nothing more I can tell you about Morgan's death."

I concentrated on the remaining ingredients and lowered the pan's heat, but I couldn't reduce my own. Johnson had me hot and bothered. He waltzed in bitching and I wanted to kiss him. Or more.

"Boy, that smells good."

"You're not getting an invitation to dinner. Why are you here?"

"You're an intelligent woman. Observant." He leaned forward, tapping his pen against the notebook. "Plus, someone tried to run you down yesterday. That means you're important to the case."

Maybe he'd get an invitation for dinner after all.

"I figure you know something you don't know you know."

Dinner invitation cancelled. Cop Sexy could get his own food. "Right. Because putting what you don't know you know into conversational English is so darn easy. I can't help you. Thanks for stopping. Bye-bye now."

He stood. "Look. I'd like to talk about what you noticed at class."

"I already gave you a statement. Isn't that enough?"

"Those were the facts. I'd like your insights. Your perceptions about the others in class."

What did the man really want?

"Women always watch each other. They see things

guys don't care, um, notice." He held his ballpoint above his notebook. "Did you see anything in particular, any negative interactions? Anything that might point to a killer?"

Sure, he stuck his foot in his mouth, but working for a construction company had toughened me up long ago. Poor guy meant well. Bless his heart. I'd help him out, right after I made him wait.

"You want anything to drink?"

"No, thanks. What do you remember from the start, when you arrived at the studio?"

I poured myself a small glass of red wine and joined him at the table. "Flash sat at the reception desk when Ginger and I arrived." A pause lengthened.

Detective Johnson raised his head. "'Flash being?"

"The stuck-up blonde."

"So?"

"So why was she filling in for Justin Nash? According to Ginger, Justin was often late and nobody sat in for him before. I didn't see him until after Morgan died." My stomach clenched. I wondered how long the memory of Morgan's death would nauseate me.

"Nash ran an errand. His alibi checks. What else?"

"Flash yelled at me for wearing my shoes."

"I'm guessing you smiled politely and removed them?"

"I wanted to flip her off." Probably shouldn't have admitted to pissed.

"Then what?"

"Morgan came out and schmoozed. And no, I didn't notice anything off."

"You sound unsure. What are you remembering?"

"Well, there were lots of small groups."

"And?"

Geez, the guy sounded like a daytime talk show host. "This is essentially a small town. We have best friends, but most of us get along with everyone. We're nice to those outside our circle. That's what I'm used to seeing at gatherings. People mingling, hugging, you know. No one did that at class. Women stood alone or with maybe one other person. The atmosphere was... cold."

"Why do you think that was?"

"I don't know. Maybe they're strangers."

My memory skittered back, not really wanting to touch on the death scene. Detective Johnson put down his pen and sat with folded hands. It was kind of nice to have somebody wait for my ideas.

"When Morgan walked into the room, the dynamics changed."

"How so?"

"Like a light went on inside some of the women. They preened and tried to get his attention. But others, they either looked stone-faced or they ignored everyone else in the room, including Morgan. I didn't think about their behavior at the time, but that's kinda strange."

He picked up his pen. "Sure is. Can you give me names?"

"Hello? I told you, the only person I knew there was Ginger." Crap. I'd just thrown him at her. "But I don't know that she noticed."

"I'll check." He stashed his pen and notebook in an inside pocket. "I appreciate your help."

"Sure. Anything else, Detective Johnson?"

"Dirk."

I tried out his name in my head. "Okay. Any more

35

questions, Dirk?"

He stood. "Not right now, Katie."

"Dirk?" He waited. "What killed Morgan?"

"I can't tell you, Katie. You know that."

"That's Ms. Sheridan to you. And I'm calling Ginger and telling her not to cooperate with you."

He breathed a sound between a sigh and a huff. "Evidence is inconclusive. We're waiting on toxicology."

"Poison? Yikes, I didn't smell almonds on his breath when I tried to resuscitate him. But then, I didn't do mouth-to-mouth."

"We ruled out cyanide. And that's all you're getting out of me." He moved to the kitchen door.

"Hey, Dirk?"

He turned and waited.

"You said someone tried to run me down yesterday. Like my accident wasn't one. How do you figure?"

"No skid marks."

"But there wouldn't be skid marks, he wasn't trying to stop."

"Exactly."

Sometimes my denseness surprises even me. "But that means ..."

Dirk's hand came up. I thought he'd touch me but he dropped his arm to his side. "You're too cute to get hurt again. Lock the damn door, Katie." My mouth continued catching flies as the door fell shut behind him.

Locking the door, I headed for the phone. I warned Ginger that Dirk lurked on her trail. Then I poured another glass of wine. Dirk seemed to be on my trail too. Boy Howdie, what a lucky girl.

****

I let the magazine drop to the floor. Inspired by the article on giving head, I turned my attention to the fine specimen in front of me. "Let's see. This says I should run my tongue up to..."

The phone rang.

"Let it go." Johnson, no, *Dirk* growled the words. His hand snaked out, his fingers grabbed the back of my neck. He pulled me against his chest and his lips attacked mine, driving me into sensory overload.

The phone kept ringing.

I pulled back. "I should get that."

Dirk's lust-filled eyes were the last image I held from my dream. I blinked, turned my head toward the end table and picked up the phone.

"Katie, are you alone?"

I sighed. "Unfortunately, yes." Although come to think on it, having a dirty dream about someone I met the day before might be safer than doing the real thing.

"Katie, I received another letter."

I jerked myself upright and leaned my head against my couch back. That second glass of wine had put me down for a nap in front of the television.

"Could Morgan have sent the note yesterday?"

"The message came hand delivered."

"Ginger, he could have arranged for delivery before..."

"I don't think so."

"Why not?"

My friend sobbed. I stood, ready to do battle.

"Katie, the note says," she inhaled, the sound loud in my ear. "It says they have Morgan's photos and the price has gone up. I'm also being threatened about Morgan's murder. The blackmailer says I have motive and opportunity."

Holy crap. "I'll be right over."

I wiped the sleep from my eyes and brushed the parts needing brushing in record time, which said something given my damaged physical state. I limped to the car Ginger loaned me over my limp protests. Even though the vehicle was her oldest, least expensive automobile, its original purchase price would've made a down payment on a hefty mortgage.

Ginger and I had been friends since kindergarten. Years later, after my parents' deaths, she kept me going. We'd do anything to protect each other and have. I was her maid of honor when she married Rob, but we were maids of honor for each other long before.

Anger spiked and churned my stomach. Ginger had made one big mistake. One, in all the years we'd hung together. Now that judgment lapse had bitten her in the backside and whoever threatened her could bite my butt. No way I'd let some sleaze take down my friend.

I turned the knob and pushed, but the door didn't open. Detective Johnson had apparently been preaching his lock-up sermon to my best friend too.

Ginger threw open the door and enfolded me in a tight hug. When we pulled apart, I saw her red-rimmed eyes and mentally cursed the blackmailer again.

"Is Rob here?"

"No. He had to go into the office."

On Sunday night? I didn't say that, but my suspicion hung in the air. "So we can talk?"

Ginger grabbed my hand and pulled me inside, turned and locked the door behind me. So much for feeling safe in the little town of Granville Falls.

"Need some coffee?"

I really wanted more wine, but I agreed to caffeine and we walked into her bright, airy kitchen. The room's renovations, planned by Ginger, reflected her warm personality and love of baking. Redolent of cinnamon and her namesake spice, the room put the kitchens in glossy decorating magazines to shame, mostly because the space was not stylized out of all personality. The only thing lacking was a kid or two. The children Ginger wanted and Rob shied from considering.

We sat. Ginger served me a mug of her dynamite decaf and followed with a plate of home-baked cookies.

"Oh good, a bedtime snack." I snagged a chocolate chip cookie. What a shame. A second cookie hid under the first. I bit and warm chocolate melted even more in my mouth. "Yum."

This wasn't a homey get-together. Ginger was in trouble, a fact rammed home when I saw she didn't join me in a sugar indulgence. She white-knuckled the coffee mug but didn't drink. My milk chocolate turned bitter.

Time to get down to business. "Where's the note?"

Ginger pulled the paper out of her pocket and handed it over with two fingers.

Wishing I didn't have to touch the nasty paper, I unfolded the communication. The demand looked like something from a detective show with words cut from magazines and newspapers.

The price for your secret is $20,000. Wait for instructions. Weasel out and the cops get the photos.

"Twenty grand? Can you get this amount without Rob finding out?"

She bowed her head and spoke to her lap. "Yes." I knew Ginger had money, but other than buying flashy cars, she didn't flaunt her wealth. Her inheritance didn't hit me in the face every minute.

I got up and moved around the table, placing my arm over her shoulders. "Aw, sweetie, I'm so sorry."

She turned her head into my shoulder and let loose. My stomach clenched with her heart-breaking sounds. I didn't move as she emptied her tear ducts.

I handed her a napkin. Something about the note bothered me, but I didn't know what.

The light clicked on. "Twenty grand? That's not much considering what you're worth. Why so little?"

Ginger hiccupped. "I didn't think of that." She hiccupped again. "Not the amount. Just that it was happening." Her eyes narrowed. "It's not much, is it? Considering. The women who take, took, classes with Morgan could afford that amount without a squabble."

The light continued to glow. Dang, I felt like the Milky Way. "It's not much from one person, but what if there is more than one of you under the blackmailer's thumb? Twenty grand times ten or even twenty people starts to add up."

My friend's eyes got big. "So Mona's story about other women is probably true?"

"Most likely. Ginger, we have to take this to the cops."

"Are you crazy? I can't go to the police. Rob will find out. Everyone in town will know. They'll believe the note's accusations that I'm a killer, not my protestations of innocence. No. Absolutely not. No way." She crossed her arms. Subject closed.

I thought back to Johnson's Sexy /A-hole Cop split

personality and realized she'd nailed the dilemma. He'd investigate. But investigating didn't mean he'd come up with the right answer.

I didn't feel comfortable but nodded my head in agreement. "We're facing a decision."

"I know."

We sighed in unison. "Guess that means the Demonic Duo is back in business."

Ginger's lips twitched. "My cape is packed away but I know where it is."

"Packed away? Mine's in the hall closet."

"Everything is in your hall closet, unless you've piled something in your living room."

"Hey, I can find anything, anytime."

The familiar banter soothed, but the tacit agreement we'd made hovered. We'd decided to catch a blackmailer.

I hoped we didn't end up like Morgan.

Chapter Five

"We need to know about Morgan's activities."

I'd stopped at Ginger's before heading to my drafting job. We sipped coffee and munched cookies, picking up where we'd left off the night before. Although I'd gone home prior to the late news, Rob hadn't returned. I didn't ask when, or if, he'd come back.

Ginger chewed her fingernail. "If Morgan saw another woman, I can't imagine who. Well, except for Brandi Wells, and that's only because of what she let slip."

"Brandi?"

Ginger grinned. "That's Flash to you."

"She has a name? I thought she'd have a serial number."

Ginger stopped chewing on her nail and chose a cookie. "Mona does owe us a truffle from Saturday."

Friends shouldn't let friends cookie alone, so I joined her. "And a slew of gossip to top it off."

Ginger grinned and reached for a bag on the chair next to her. She pulled out a black cape with a flourish. "The Demonic Duo rides again."

I stood and pulled my cape from my oversize bag. The garment settled around my shoulders. I felt invincible. At least at that moment. "Let's hit the Chocolate Fix after I get off work."

Ginger rubbed her fingers over the shiny rayon

cape. "We had no clue how tough life could get, did we?" Her fingers stilled. "Life seemed so easy the last time we wore these."

I grabbed another cookie. "We can turn the blackmail notes over to the cops, you know."

Her frown gave me her answer. "I'm going to pay the $20,000. It'll save my marriage."

My jaw ached from being clamped shut. Didn't seem like there was much to save.

****

The Get Solid Builders trailer stood empty when I arrived at work. My scraped palms made typing difficult, and I couldn't do much else. Not to mention the old trailer creaked with heavy wind gusts. I didn't feel comfortable or secure. I left a note for my boss, Jim Prestwick, and returned to Ginger's house.

I'd barely pulled onto her driveway before she was out her door and in the car with me. We walked into the Chocolate Fix, not surprised to find the aromatic store almost empty mid-afternoon.

Mona looked up from stocking her glass-fronted showcase. "Hey, girls, what's up? Didn't think I'd see you in here today."

"Actually, we came in for that truffle you owe us. And some gossip."

Mona winked before picking out a selection of confections and walking around the counter. "Let's get down to it, ladies. My favorite thing, besides chocolate, is gossip."

We settled at a table.

"Mona," I began, "what did you mean when you said Morgan rode for a fall?"

She snorted. "He wasn't riding for a fall, he flirted

with disaster and got screwed. Let me tell you what I know."

We all glanced over our shoulders and moved our heads closer together. Even though we were the only people in the store.

"I know he slept with married women exclusively."

"You know this, how?"

Mona waved her had in answer.

I avoided Ginger's gaze. "Any long term affairs?"

"Nah, not unless you count two weeks as long term. He'd hit up lonely or abused women. Jerkface had infallible radar. He never made a mistake. Never chose a happily married woman. At least, not that I heard."

Ginger shifted in her seat. I struggled to keep from looking at her.

"Nope, he knew how to play women," Mona continued.

I was confused. "That's more Jerry Springer than CSI."

"Bastard didn't stop with seduction. He branched out, started to hit up his girlfriends for money."

A chill ran down my back. "How do you know all this?"

Mona leaned back in her chair and crossed her arms. "I know someone—and I'm not giving a name— who cashed in part of her retirement fund to buy Morgan a luxury Swiss-made watch." She tilted her head then shook it. "Woman said it was a gift because he helped her out. Helped her out of a chunk of cash, that's for sure."

I leaned forward, unable to sit still. "Do you know about gifts from other women?"

Mona popped a truffle in her mouth and chewed.

"You bet. After my friend gave Morgan the watch, I heard other women gave him expensive toys, clothes, paid his studio rent, you name it."

"Do you think he blackmailed any of the women?"

Mona stopped mid chew. "What, you think the gifts were given willingly?" She snorted. "Not hardly." She finished chewing and swallowed. "Actually, the first gifts were in response to casual hints Morgan dropped in conversation. After he dumped a woman, the demands got worse."

She picked up another truffle. We waited for her to finish. Her vigorous chewing told me she'd chosen a caramel.

"My friend said she received a note after Morgan left her. He'd detailed the exact watch brand and model he wanted, in white gold, and said he'd appreciate a good-bye gift from her. She laughed until she turned over the note."

Mona studied the plate of truffles but didn't make a move. When she looked at me, her eyes were filled with tears.

"Bastard had a photo of them in bed. Doing the deed." She sniffed. We waited.

"Funny enough, you can see my friend's face full on, but Morgan, not so much."

"It was more important to show the woman because she has the most to lose." Ginger's voice sounded shaky and quiet. "If her husband sees the picture, he can't go after Morgan because he doesn't have proof of the guy's identity. He can divorce his cheating wife and keep everything in the settlement. The only ones who lose are the women."

Another light went on. "He hated women."

Mona shook her head. "Poetic justice."

We exchanged glances.

She continued. "I mean, he died surrounded by women."

Suddenly his death seemed a whole lot more complicated than I had realized. And it didn't look as if Ginger was in the clear. Someone had picked up where Morgan's death left off. Unless he'd had a partner in blackmail all along.

I hurried my next words. "Mona, can you give us any names? Other than your friend's?"

"Well, the flashy blonde in here yesterday was one of Morgan's latest."

Ginger sat forward. "Brandi Wells?"

"Yep, that sounds right. Snooty as all get out. A real rich bitch. Jealous too." Mona looked at me. "She said you tried to make time with Morgan."

"What?" My cheeks turned red hot, but not from embarrassment.

"She made it sound like you killed him because he wouldn't give you the time of day." Mona studied me.

"I met the man yesterday. Sure, he was hunky, but I didn't want to bed him and I sure didn't kill him."

"Hell, back in the sixties, you could screw someone you just met, no problem. Never mind. You don't need my remembrances." Mona's gaze held mine. She seemed to come to a decision. "You don't have murder in your aura. At least, not sneaky murder. Your victim would see death coming."

Aura? Not sure if she'd given me a compliment or not, I changed the subject. "So, how much did the watch cost?"

"A cool twenty-five grand. I wonder who

inherits?"

Ginger put down a half-eaten truffle. "I can tell you one thing—the heir won't be a woman."

****

The alarm rang way too early the following morning. I pulled myself out of bed and into the shower, not at all happy I faced another workday. Don't get me wrong, I love my job, but yesterday hadn't been relaxing. Not to mention the weekend had been a real killer.

I winced at my lame humor and stumbled into the kitchen. Standing in the doorway, I wondered what was wrong with the picture. I finally realized the overhead light shone in my face. The strong smell of burnt coffee filled the room. I blinked.

Brown liquid dripped from the machine I'd programmed last night, but no carafe collected the stream. Coffee trickled down the cabinet front and pooled on the floor. The carafe sat on the table with a note attached. I pulled the plug on my coffeemaker and checked the door lock.

Unlocked. I knew I'd turned the bolt the night before. I remembered checking it. So how did someone get in? Rubbing my arms, I skirted the kitchen table and headed for the front door. That door was locked. Maybe I only locked one door, but that didn't compute. My familiar, beloved house felt more than a little creepy.

The note waited, taunting me with its presence. I picked it up with two fingers. The message read short but not sweet.

Tell your friend to pay the money and keep your mouths shut.

Looked like Morgan had had a partner. Minus my

promise to keep Ginger's secret, I'd call that big ole bad boy Dirk over for security detail. Instead, wide awake and knees quivering, I mopped up the mess. Someone needed money. And was desperate. Not a good combination.

I rushed through dressing with shaky fingers. Feeling like Adrian Monk, television's favorite obsessive-compulsive detective, I flipped my door lock three times, jiggling the knob each time. Part of me wanted to sit with a loaded gun (which I didn't own) and wait for the intruder. The other part wanted to run long, hard, and far, far away.

Far, far away won the toss. I motored across town to the Get Solid Builders trailer. The crew supervisors and the routine morning briefing waited for me.

I closed my eyes. Shoot. I'd forgotten to bring the doughnuts.

"Want some coffee, Katie? I brought doughnuts."

Jim Prestwick shoved a mug and some deep-fried dough into my hands. His voice was low. "Sorry I missed you yesterday. We heard about the pretzel guy. You okay?"

Translation: pretzel guy meant yoga teacher in construction guy speak. Morgan.

I blinked back tears. Jim liked people to believe he was a hard-ass but he stood first in line to help anyone in trouble.

"Yep, thanks. I'm fine." And puppies fly.

He turned toward the assembled supervisors and raised his voice. "You're just in time. We need your input."

My throat clearing took longer than it should have. "What do you need?"

"Well, Cam just announced he's gonna pop the question."

No news there. Cam supervised our finish carpenters. His girlfriend had been after his ass for two years. I was just surprised she took so long to nail him down. "Congrats, Cam."

Cam, a tall man with a dark blond brush cut, Slavic cheekbones and puppy-dog eyes, displayed his dimples and saluted me.

"So we want to know. Should he pop the question at her apartment, get down on his knees, that whole outdated bit, or rent a billboard? I told him I know someone in outdoor advertising who'll give him a deal on a moving electronic board ad over on I-40."

What was more harmful? Eating a doughnut or pinching myself black and blue to determine if I dreamed? I chose the doughnut. Chewing bought me time to form a response.

"We figure you're female and you've been married, so you're the one to ask."

"Gee, thanks for making me part of the project, guys." With everyone's gaze on me, I bit off a big chunk of fried dough and chewed.

"Well?" Jim put his hands on his hips.

I swallowed. "Apartment. Definitely the apartment. Bring a bunch of her favorite flowers, cold champagne and chocolate. You'll be a hero."

Cam smiled. "Thanks, Katie."

His relieved look told me Jim had pushed the electronic sign idea.

"Sure. Get one of the candy boxes from Chocolate Fix and give her the ring in that. She'll think you're Adonis and her favorite movie star all rolled into one."

"Got it."

"And whatever you do, don't tell her you asked these yahoos for advice on proposing. Let her think you came up with the grand gesture on your own."

"I don't want to lie, Katie."

"You're not. You're just not telling her everything. It's called presenting yourself in your best light."

The group hooted out suggestions. Jim started the meeting. I listened on autopilot while my mind moved in strange directions.

Ginger told me Morgan had always presented himself in the best light. She'd said he appeared humble while making women think adoration was his due. He talked a spiritual game, played a material one.

An idea lurked. When I reached for the thought, the impression disappeared. Was the blackmail Morgan's game or did he have a partner? How many women did he play? Who threatened Ginger, a possible partner or an opportunist? Either way, Ginger was in trouble. The cops couldn't learn about the blackmail note or she'd be suspect number one. Worse, she'd never be able to keep the truth from her husband.

I understood Ginger's harassment, but why was someone after me? I could take care of myself, but knowing someone entered my home while I slept gave me the heebie-jeebies. The pain medication I'd taken probably kept me from waking, but still. Made me think twice about living alone. I'd be stopping on my way home to buy new deadbolts.

After my divorce, friendly though it was, I was gun shy. I didn't want kids, but a relationship would be good. Yeah, I was ready for that. Maybe. With a good guy. Unless my relationship wish came from a reaction to the break-in. Crap.

Dirk Johnson's' good looks came to mind followed by flashes of his sexy bod. Wait. What? No, no, no. He reminded me too much of my ex, Chris. Bossy as shit.

My perverse brain, high on sugar, wouldn't back off. Oh, no. Instead, I visualized a rating sheet, with Dirk heading Column A and Chris topping Column B. The tick marks started to pile up and the boys ran even on the looks, hot body and hard worker lines. I thought about the less obvious things like sense of humor, generosity, consideration and sharing. Dirk remained a dark horse, but my mental pencil wanted to give him points for those. Wishful thinking, probably. Chris's self-absorption skewed my take on men. Any interest my ex showed masked a need to control my entire life. The only friend Chris hadn't chased away was Ginger.

Dirk looked better and better. But I'd been down that road. It was a dead end. A cul-de-sac of errors.

I made up my mind. A relationship could wait.

Meanwhile, another part of my brain decided I should report the break-in. There was no reason Dirk or Matt had to know—the intruder had nothing to do with Morgan's death. Or Ginger's blackmail. I needed a sense of security. I'd call as soon as the meeting ended. The cops would have a hard time finding the creep who invaded my privacy, but I couldn't let the situation go. Especially given my worries about being a suspect in Morgan's death. I felt stalked, and if reporting a break-in gave me peace, so be it.

I turned my attention back to the meeting. And work. With thoughts of Dirk interrupting more than I liked.

Chapter Six

The trailer door squeaked open. I didn't bother to look up. "Jim, I told you. The plans will be ready at 2:15 and not a minute earlier."

"It's not Jim and you're pretty exact. How can you guarantee that specific time?"

The man had been flitting around my thoughts all morning but I didn't expect Dirk to show up at my job. I plastered on a phony smile. "Detective Johnson. What brings you to my high-rise office?"

He slammed his palms down on my desk. My computer screen shook, but I almost didn't notice. Our gazes tangled and his pupils grew larger, taking over most of his irises.

"Hey, be careful. That's an expensive piece of equipment you just shook up, *Dirk*."

"What is wrong with you?" His face darkened. He inhaled, seeming to capture all the office's air. "I told you to lock your damn house. Why can't you understand there's a killer in town and you're in his or her sights?"

I stood, needing any advantage I could garner against the looming, angry cop. My hands took up a "don't mess with me" position on each hip. I leaned forward, my nose close to his. "There's nothing wrong with me. I heard you perfectly and I locked my door. What's your problem?"

He mimicked my tone. "My problem?" He crossed his arms, probably to keep from strangling me. "My problem is that you had a break-in and didn't call me or Matt. Are you covering for someone or something?"

"Oh." I hadn't expected Dirk to hear about the break-in. Silly me. The police force is fairly large but Granville Falls is still a small town. Don't know how I forgot that.

"You're on burglary now? Let's see...the Departments of Homicide, Traffic, Burglary—you're a one man police force."

His expression made me rethink my snarky answer. "The break-in didn't seem like such a big deal." My voice slipped and the bravado I'd thought I could project proved a no show. "I've already bought new deadbolt locks."

"No big deal?" His voice echoed off the trailer walls. "The guys called me in after you left. I could still smell the burnt coffee. The creep levered a window. They found traces of footprints but couldn't get a solid impression." He shook his head. "When are you going to wise up?"

"I told you. I'll take care of the locks when I get home."

"And the windows?"

He made Chris seem copasetic.

"I'll secure those too. What's with you?"

"The coffee pot was set up to scare you. And I don't want you or any other woman getting hurt on my watch."

His eyes held a spark of hurt and something more, an expression I didn't understand. It hinted at pride and fear. Whatever drove him had some age to it.

"So you came over here to bitch at me?" I watched him visibly re-grasp his control.

"No, I didn't."

My blood sugar had dropped, I had a deadline, and I felt feisty. "So, what is it then? I've got a project to finish."

"I have questions about someone connected with the case."

My stomach dropped. I'd like tearing Flash apart with him, but I didn't think that was his primary agenda. Not if my trusty gut instinct proved right.

"Sorry, don't have time right now. How about next week?"

"How about tonight?"

"You know, I have a bunch of D.I.Y. work tonight. There's a hard-ass on my case about securing my house."

"I know my way around a drill. I'll bring some tools. We can talk while I help you install the locks."

"That's really not a good idea."

His hazel eyes darkened again. He leaned closer to me. "Got something better in mind?"

Dirk's gaze dropped to my lips and my hormones shrieked out x-rated suggestions having to do with drilling holes and screwdrivers. I licked my lips afraid whatever came out of my mouth next would be a double entendre.

The door slammed open. "Katie, where the hell are those plans? I needed the damn things yesterday."

Tension swirled thick but Jim didn't seem to notice. He raked a glare over Dirk. "Who are you? You better not be screwing around with Katie. I need her head together."

"No, sir, I'm not." The cop's voice dropped for my ears only. "Unless she wants me to."

Dirk eased past Jim and stopped at the door. "See you later, Ms. Sheridan."

Jim jerked a thumb in the direction of the door. "Who's he?"

"Cop. Wants to ask me more questions about the...pretzel guy."

"He gives you any grief, tell me. I'll get the mayor to bust his ass."

That's the thing about Jim. He'd call City Hall in a heartbeat. He put his meaty paw on my shoulder. "Katie, you had a rough weekend. You know if I didn't need you on this project I'd let you have more time off?"

"No problem, boss. I can handle everything."

"If you can't, you'll tell me, right?" Jim's a sweetie, but he doesn't understand women.

"You bet." I turned to my desk and picked up part of the plans. "I have most of this done. Why don't you take what I have and tell me the changes you need?"

Jim patted my shoulder again, grabbed the papers and seated himself at his desk. My thoughts jumped. Dirk seemed interested in me, but he probably wanted to talk about Ginger tonight, if he really showed. I had my doubts about him coming over.

If I didn't have locks to install at home, I'd find someplace else to be, just in case Dirk followed up on his threat to show with tools, experience and questions.

****

I stepped inside my kitchen and wished I hadn't.

Dirk had been right. The smell of burnt coffee lingered like a hangover's bad taste. But that wasn't what made the hair stand up on the back of my neck.

Looking around, nothing seemed out of place, but my house looked too neat. Someone had been searching, and not well.

My feet wouldn't move, which could have been a bad or a good thing. Tuning in, I opened up to my surroundings. The house seemed quiet, no creaking boards or odd drafts. A good sign in my old bungalow. The place seemed empty, but I wanted to make sure.

I'm no hero, so I grabbed my phone, setting it to quick dial 9-1-1 with one touch. I picked up an iron skillet in the other hand and tiptoed through the house. Throwing open closet doors with both hands full was hellish, but I managed. Fifteen minutes later, I took my first real breath since coming home. No one hid under my bed but the energy imprint of my intruder left a nasty feel.

Foregoing my usual post-work glass of merlot, I started dinner even though I wasn't hungry. Preparing food gave my shaky hands something to do and leftovers meant no chopping or dicing.

Dinner heated on the stove, giving me time to replace the kitchen door lock. My hands still weren't steady so the job took longer than expected. A loud creak on the back stairs made me drop the screwdriver.

"You should check your pot. Dinner's starting to burn."

Shoot. Dirk smiled down at me. I had to fight my hormones *again*. My overheated reactions were tiresome. I rescued my leftovers and turned to see Dirk inspecting the doorjamb.

His thumb rubbed a scratch and he drilled me with his gaze. "These gouge marks weren't here earlier. Did someone break in again?"

"No. My hand slipped."

"Sweetheart, don't even try lying to me. Prevarication doesn't work for career criminals and won't work for you. Your hands shake like a bad case of palsy and you jump when I get too close."

I bit my lower lip. Dirk's eyes darkened. "It's silly."

"The only thing silly is you not telling me what happened."

"I'm nervous because it *feels* like someone searched my house while I was at work."

His gaze sharpened. "I suppose you picked up a frying pan and went looking for trouble."

How did he know? "My speed dial was set to 9-1-1."

"That's a great help when you're bleeding out from a gunshot wound."

"The house felt empty."

"Famous last words. Anything missing?"

I shook my head. "It's just that everything looked too neat. Neater than when I left this morning."

The guy deserved credit. He didn't roll his eyes and I could tell he considered my words. "You're sure?"

This time my head moved in the positive.

He nodded. "Okay. Let's get the locks installed."

That was all he said yet I fell halfway in love. Dirk picked up the other lock and headed for the front door. My hands were better but still shaky. He finished installing his lock the same time I completed mine.

"Want some dinner?" I asked.

He glanced to the stove. Following his glance, I saw the pot smoking.

"Damn. I hate when that happens."

Dirk had enough sense not to say a word, a tick mark on my score sheet for him. Instead, he pulled out his phone. "Pizza okay?"

I nodded.

"Sausage or pepperoni?"

"Both."

He grinned. Dirk placed the order and hung up with a graceful economy of motion. "Pizza will take about forty minutes. Let's start on the windows."

Dirk didn't say why he'd really come to my bungalow and I kept my mouth shut. We worked together like a seasoned team—a scary thought. We finished the last of the ground floor windows before the pizza guy rang the bell.

"Beer?"

He hesitated and then he nodded. "Sure."

I hooked two longnecks from the fridge. The paper plates and napkins were already on the table. We dug in.

Two inhaled pieces later, I reached for a third and he broached his first question.

"So you're divorced?" His gaze stayed on the pizza, so I couldn't get a take on why he asked.

My appetite dissipated. "The split was friendly, if that's what you're wondering. We exchanged birthday and Christmas cards for a while. That died out, but you know, the cards were a gesture."

"What kind of gesture?"

I pondered for several heartbeats. "Probably a sign of 'no hard feelings.' Like we declared a permanent truce instead of all out war."

"Where is he now?"

"Another mindset in a different state. Texas maybe.

We grew apart."

"So he wouldn't have come by here today while you were out?"

"Right. Couldn't be him." I picked up my pizza but didn't take a bite. "What about you? Married?"

"Divorced. All out warfare. She got custody of the kids and most of what we bought together."

I figured he got the bills, but he didn't go there, so I didn't either.

"I miss the kids, but they're better off without me."

I replaced the pizza and pushed my plate away. "That's a load of self-serving crap."

"No, really. Their stepfather is loaded. They spend time together as a family. It's cool."

His expression looked anything but cool. Listening to my intuition for a change, I didn't pursue the topic, which was fine because he looked ready to drop a bomb. Guess I pissed him off.

"Mind if I have another beer?"

I pointed to the fridge. "Help yourself." There's no law against watching a fine ass bending over to find one of the bottles I'd left on the bottom shelf, so I indulged. He straightened and I jerked my gaze back to the plate in front of me.

"Opener?"

"Drawer on the left next to the stove." Too late, I remembered where I'd stashed the latest written threat. "Wait, I'll get the opener. That drawer is a mess."

He looked up from the open drawer with a grin. "No problem. I'm an investigator.

"What's this?" His quiet tone surprised me until my brain processed his timbre. Pissed and getting more pissed.

Always the optimist, I stalled. "What's what? Can't find the bottle opener?"

Dirk pointed. "When were you going to tell me about the note?"

"What note?" My angry tone sounded real, probably because I was pissed. At myself.

He looked at me, just looked, and I steeled my backbone.

"You're not being honest and this is a murder investigation. Does that note refer to Ginger?"

The mutinous look I practiced through my teen years didn't work. He waited for my answer. When I didn't reply, he changed direction.

"What was Ginger's relation to the deceased?"

My hand jumped before I could stop it. Damn him. I fell officially out of love and erased all his tick marks from the good column.

"She attended classes at the center. I don't think it was more than that."

He sighed and I almost sighed with him. I really was a pathetic liar. "Promise me you'll be discreet."

"Does the note refer to Ginger?"

"Tell me you won't talk to her in front of her husband. Not that he's ever home, but still."

"Answer me. Does the note mean that Ginger's being blackmailed?" He paused. "I can speak with her when her husband isn't there."

I noticed he didn't promise discretion, but I knew I'd gotten all the concessions he'd give. I inhaled like I hadn't breathed in the last three minutes. Maybe I hadn't.

"Ginger received a blackmail note demanding twenty thousand dollars."

Dirk sat down and led me through a set of questions that might have been painless if they were about someone other than my best friend.

"You understand I can't let this go, right?"

I nodded, too miserable to get snarky. "She couldn't have killed Morgan. Ginger made a mistake, but she's not violent. Whoever did this is underhanded." I'd been wondering if Rob had killed Morgan out of jealousy and hoped Dirk didn't suspect Rob too.

"Preliminary autopsy results indicate poison. Poison is often a woman's weapon."

"Ginger isn't a murderer." I thrust my chin out and kept my posture unbent. "She wouldn't even know where to get poison."

His gaze chilled me. "Do you?"

"What kind?"

He unfolded himself from the chair and stood looking down at me. I felt like a Lilliputian. Dirk ran the back of his fingers across my cheek. I shivered. Holding my chin in his grasp, he gently pulled my head up. Our lips were too close for words and I hoped he'd kiss me.

"Don't be foolish. Call me if you or Ginger get another note."

His fingers brushed heat against my lips and he left.

****

Ginger howled. No other word described the noise coming from my receiver. "You told him!"

"I didn't say a word. He found the note in my drawer."

Somehow I doubted the difference meant anything to my friend.

"You let him find it."

This conversation was hurting both of us when talking was supposed to help. "I didn't, but that's not the point. He's coming to talk with you, and you need to be prepared." My cheek still tingled where his fingers had brushed my skin. "He's sneaky. He'll ask you hard questions and make them seem like everyday stuff. Get yourself together, Ginger."

A hiccup sounded. Crap. "Can you come over?"

My body sent out a dry-throat alert. "Not possible. I'm afraid he's looking for a reason to haul me into the station. Interfering with an investigation would give him cause."

"Huh. I bet Cop Sexy wants to do a full body search. He wouldn't have to take you to the station for that."

Not a discussion I wanted to have, but at least my friend focused on something other than the note. "Oh, give me a break. He's not into me. Not at all."

"He should be. You're gorgeous, smart, loyal." Her last word broke.

"Yeah, just like a Border collie. Our coloring is the same, seeing as I'm white with black hair. My eyes are brown, though, not that spooky blue some of those dogs have."

"Oh, stop."

Good. Ginger had fallen for the distraction and warmed to "let's match Katie up" mode. Not my favorite topic, but if discussing possible mates relaxed her, the ploy worked.

"You have big bones but you're not fat. And you keep yourself toned. If you didn't, you'd never have gotten through class on Saturday."

I hadn't known so many muscles were required in a stretch. The women in class made the poses look easy, but a lot of strength was required to practice yoga effortlessly. Those skinny women were seriously strong.

My breath stuck in my lungs, waiting to see if Ginger would break down again. An inhalation that would do a yoga master proud echoed over the phone line.

"So you're not a stick figure like Flash. Real women have curves."

This spoken by a willowy blonde. "You're making soap company commercials now?"

"Cop Sexy talked to you longer than anyone else. And he looked at you. Really looked when you walked out. Let me tell you, I know interest when I see it, and he's interested. In you."

My psyche leaped in joy with her words. I ignored my inner self. "He wanted to figure out if his handcuffs would fit me."

"Ooh, I didn't know you were into kinky stuff. When were you going to tell me?"

Ginger's teasing meant she felt better. I hated to bring her down, but she needed a wake-up call. "Sweetie, sorry to remind you, but he's on his way, and you need to tell him everything."

"But—"

"Everything. Don't hold back."

"The story will get out and Rob..."

"He doesn't deserve you, but let's stay focused. Detective Johnson already knows about the note. If you're truthful, he'll be more inclined to believe you're innocent. Then he'll look for the real killer."

Deep silence could be a little scary. I sat at the edge of my chair.

"Okay, I'll talk with him."

Her doorbell sounded. My gut told me Dirk waited.

"Just remember he's sneaky. I'll come over in a bit so you can fill me in after Johnson leaves."

I heard the snick of her dead bolt just before she said goodbye. The sound twisted my gut into a knot. I hoped Ginger was home when I got there and not at the police station waiting for bail.

Chapter Seven

My normal path to Ginger's took me past the Yoga
Studio. I'd planned that excuse if I got stopped or seen
by one sexy cop named Dirk Johnson.

The studio lights shone onto the sidewalk, a real
surprise given the crime scene tape strung around the
place. A black and white sat parked out front. Justin
Nash leaned against the side of the car. His slumped
shoulders, crossed arms and bent head gave me all the
hints I needed about his attitude.

My decision to snoop came without conscious
thought. I pulled into a nearby parking space and got
out. When I reached Justin, I held out my right hand.

"Justin, isn't it? My name is Katie Sheridan. Last
Saturday was my first class, but I'm so sorry about what
happened."

When my outstretched hand wasn't grasped by
Justin in return, I dropped my arm and waited for him
to look at me. He didn't.

He lifted his head. His naked hatred made me step
back. "I hear confession is good for the soul."

"Are you implying something? I don't...I didn't
know Morgan. I had no reason to want him dead. I
understand your grief. I just stopped to extend
sympathy."

"Oh, really?" He crossed his arms across a muscled
chest covered with a tight black tee. "I heard you were

kneeling next to Morgan right before he died. That you touched him, spoke with him. Then you left and when you came back, you made it seem like you tried to save him."

My throat was so dry the swallows I attempted didn't lubricate anything.

"That's not true. I told you, I didn't know Morgan and I didn't do any of those things." My voice squeaked. The memory of death under my fingertips rushed back, making speech impossible.

Justin dropped his arms but leaned forward slightly. Somehow that seemed a bigger threat. His intense sapphire-colored eyes contrasted badly with his red face. Not to mention, blue like that isn't found in nature.

"Can you prove that? Otherwise, your tall tale is nothing but a story."

"I don't know why someone is spreading stories about me. They're not true." But a sudden thought made a very good reason clear. Blame me, the real killer walks. "Do you know who started the story that I knelt and spoke with Morgan?"

"What, I tell and you kill the eye witness?"

My temper climbed and I struggled to pull my ire under control. "I understand you don't know me, but I have no motive, and I didn't take the opportunity to kill anyone. Murder isn't in me."

His gaze moved over my body, leaving a creepy crawly feeling behind. "Well, I wasn't at the studio when the crime happened, so I wouldn't know."

My voice sounded loud. "I didn't do it. I just want to know who accused me so I can find out why."

A warm feeling covered my back and I knew

without looking Dirk stood close.

"Why don't you leave investigating to the police, Ms. Sheridan?"

I whirled and faced Dirk. My stomach clenched when I saw his stern expression. "Why don't you find out who's smearing my name? Seems to me, that's a good clue to the killer."

"We're investigating every lead, Ms. Sheridan. Thorough investigation takes time."

Justin snorted. "Time? How much time? How long will you keep the studio closed? I've got personal belongings in there, stuff I need."

Dirk gave Justin a cool look. "We're finishing up tonight. You can open tomorrow."

"The studio won't open, not without Morgan. I just want my things and for you to find the killer." He crossed his arms again and threw a glare in my direction. "Should be easy. She's standing right next to you."

The blood drained from my head. I swayed before catching my balance. The stunned feeling remained.

Detective Johnson rode to the rescue, kinda. "I'm interested in hearing how the victim's business partner knows the killer's identity. Unless your convenient alibi away from the studio doesn't hold true. Care to enlighten me?"

Justin's pout would have been cute on a two-year-old. "I'm just repeating what I heard, that's all."

"Well, keep your repetition to yourself. This is an ongoing investigation. If you have evidence, bring it to me."

Dirk switched his angry look from Justin. Yep, as I imagined, his intensity made me feel like a bug facing an entomologist. "And that includes you, Ms. Sheridan. Leave the investigation to me."

"I am. I only stopped to give Justin my condolences." A sniff escaped before I could stop expressing my disdain. "Not that he accepted them."

I turned away but my temper encouraged further confrontation. "Justin, whether you believe me or not, I didn't kill Morgan. I'm sorry he died." I caught his gaze. "I did try to save him."

Justin's expression glazed over. His shoulders shook and I moved away. Joining in on a good cry isn't my forte, even if Justin would appreciate my participation.

Ten steps later, a firm grip stopped my forward progress. Dirk.

"Katie, you mean well, but you have to stay away from the principals."

His words didn't take long to sink in, along with disbelief. "So I'm the main suspect? Why? I didn't even know the man."

"We are investigating all leads at this time."

I looked at the man who had eaten pizza at my house and helped me install locks earlier. He didn't look familiar anymore.

"Including me."

His jaw tightened. "Yes, including you."

"Do I need a lawyer?"

His hesitation said more than words.

"Just shut your mouth. You don't say anything to me. Not now. Not later. I'll get a lawyer. You can talk to him. Or her."

His silence as I left told me I had more trouble ahead. My gut instinct agreed.

****

Ginger pulled open the door, eyes puffy. "Come on in. Rob won't be home for another half hour."

"He's working late again?"

She hesitated then nodded and closed the door behind me. We headed to our kitchen hangout. Ginger set the table with tea mugs and a plate of our favorite cookies. I grabbed a tea bag and tore it open, only to feel Ginger's hand on mine.

"Katie, put that down. You hate green tea."

I threw the bag onto the table and focused on making a choice from the basket in front of me. I was more rattled than I thought. Ginger selected a chamomile tea bag and handed the paper wrapped packet to me. Guess my upset was obvious.

I took a deep breath and tackled a question I'd put off asking. "Does Rob know about Morgan?"

My friend gave a small laugh. "Are you kidding? Maybe he doesn't want to make love with me but God forbid any other man would. He'd kill the guy then he'd kill me."

She stopped and stared at me. Her face paled. "You don't think?" She took a deep breath. "No, that's not possible and I won't entertain the idea."

We sat in silence for a few minutes, but the quiet wasn't our usual peaceful companionship. I broke the awkward pause.

"So what happened with your police interview? The session couldn't have lasted long."

Ginger poured hot water into our mugs. The scent of herbal tea wafted up. I grabbed a cookie and munched while my friend remained silent. Our gazes met across the table. Mine hopeful, hers, not so much.

"Actually, the questioning went better than I expected."

"Did it?"

"I told Detective Johnson everything. The fling with Morgan and the blackmail note."

"What did he say?"

"He took one long look around the living room and asked why I thought the blackmail amount was so low." She paused. "I told him what you said, that someone must be scheming to hit multiple victims."

My breath started again. "Did Dirk ah, Detective Johnson buy that theory?"

Ginger smirked, but on her the expression looked good. Everything looked good on her. Damn it all. "First name basis, huh? Nice work."

"Just answer me, Miss Smarty-Pants."

"Dirk," the brat emphasized his name, "seemed to think that made sense."

"Anything else?"

"Not really." She tilted her head to the side, a move that indicated she thought something through. "I didn't realize it at the time, but he asked me a bunch of questions about you." She faced me. "Told you he's interested."

My heart sank right down to my feet. I could feel my blood pumper drop like a run-away elevator. Given his stern behavior at the studio, he'd gotten something else out of his conversation with Ginger.

"Do you happen to remember details?"

Something about my expression reached my friend. "What? What's wrong?"

"What kind of questions did he ask? Please, think back."

Ginger went into head tilt mode again, this time with a frown. "He just asked how long we've known each other. How we got the Demonic Duo name. Why two such disparate people are friends."

Her frown deepened and she looked scared. My voice hit scream volume. "What, what?"

My friend took a deep breath and looked sad. "I told him we've been protecting each other since second grade."

Our gazes met and held. I could tell we were thinking the same thing. Motive and opportunity. I had them both.

****

A heavy knock at the door woke me. Disoriented, I raised my nose and sniffed but didn't smell smoke. My clock read five-thirty, so I pulled a pillow over my head before I became jolted alert. Normally, if a problem is happening before I'm awake, I don't want to know. That was before the recent break-ins.

Then the knocking started again. "Police, open up. We have a warrant."

I looked out my bedroom window. Sure enough, a black and white sat in my drive with an unmarked behind the squad. Didn't take hours of watching crime show television to know an officer guarded each door. The pounding resumed.

"Hold it to yourself, will ya? I'm coming. Just give me a minute."

Grabbing my oldest, rattiest bathrobe, well, my only robe to be honest, I stumbled for the front door and threw it open.

"Detective Johnson. Just who I wanted to wake up with this morning."

The nearest policeman grinned. He looked like a boy I knew in middle school. He slanted a look at Dirk and his mirth disappeared. I checked the officer's name badge. Yep, the cop was Allen. Wow, he'd filled out. My observations took a backseat when I saw the look in Dirk's eyes.

"Ms. Kathryn Sheridan, we have a warrant to search your premises. Will you allow us to enter and carry out the warrant?"

"What? What are you looking for? You're kidding, right?"

Dirk handed me the warrant. I stumbled through the legalese. I wished I'd made time to call a lawyer. "Botanical based poison? Ricin? What the hell is that? I don't know what you're looking for, but I bet it's not here."

He didn't look at me, just pushed past. The other officers followed his lead. Allen was the last to file past my bewildered self. He took pity on me. "You always sucked in science. Castor beans, Katie. Simple, ordinary castor beans. Got any?"

My brain refused to work. "I don't even have the oil. Or am I thinking of cod liver oil?" I shook my head "Either way, no."

"I hope not, Katie. I really hope we don't find any."

I sank into the nearest chair, holding my robe closed with shaking hands. Coffee was the answer. Too bad no one asked the question but me. I watched the search for a few minutes then realized I was all but buck-naked in a house full of men.

"Hey, Allen, mind if I get dressed?"

He grinned. "Can I watch?" Yep, same old Allen.

He waved me on my way. I scooted off, grabbed

clothes from my bedroom chair and locked myself into the bathroom. A quick use of the toothpaste and hairbrush later, I returned to the living room with my heart in my throat. Really, I could feel it there, blocking my air intake.

Allen and I exchanged old home week stories for a few minutes, but that didn't help my stress level. Dirk walked into the room and breathing became more difficult. Standing over me, he crossed his arms. His taciturn face told me I inhabited one heck of a nightmare. He gestured toward the chair across from me.

"May I sit? I have a few questions."

My voice didn't work, what with my throat all closed up, so I nodded. Dirk's cold, formal demeanor scared me. A lot.

"What do you know about botanical poisons?"

"Nothing. Well, except that Allen told me you're here looking for castor beans."

Dirk's look sent Allen scurrying from the room.

"We suspect ricin, or some form of botanical poison killed Morgan Anderson last Saturday. Care to revise your story?"

"I don't have a story. I don't know what you're talking about. I don't have castor beans." And the final don't. "I don't have a reason to change anything I've told you. I'm innocent."

Good thing I wasn't a criminal because his disbelieving look had me wanting to throw myself on the mercy of the court. Sheesh. He excelled at his job.

One of the officers called Dirk into the kitchen and I sat alone pondering my fate. Castor beans are poisonous? Who knew? All I did know for sure was that I didn't possess the seeds or beans or whatever they were. I didn't even have lettuce in my refrigerator.

Dirk walked in so quietly he stood next to me before I realized he was there. He held up an evidence bag holding another plastic bag with a half inch of powder in the bottom. "Is this yours?"

Still unable to speak, I shook my head no.

Then he showed me another evidence bag holding several typewritten pages. "What about these papers?"

Again, a head shake answer.

"Ms. Sheridan, we are taking you in for questioning regarding the murder of Morgan Anderson. If you feel you need a lawyer, you may call one from the station." He held out a hand. "Come with me, please?"

"What, you're not reading me my rights?"

"You're not under arrest." The unstated "yet" hovered like an armed bomb. I stood. My stomach dropped with gravity. My legs wobbled me toward the door. Dirk walked on one side and another officer flanked me. As if Jell-O legs could take off running.

Half my neighbors pretended to pick up newspapers that hadn't arrived yet and the others looked out their windows. I ducked into the backseat of the cruiser before anyone could do that embarrassing hand-on-top-of-the-head thing to me.

At the station, Allen opened my door and we entered together. He set me up at Dirk's desk with a cup of the worst coffee I'd ever tasted.

Dirk sat and watched me grimace my way through another sip of synthetic java. "That's from the night crew. If you wait a few minutes, someone will make a new pot."

"Will the new batch be any better?"

"Not really."

I pushed the paper cup to the side. "Why did you pull me in? No, wait, why did you stage a search so early in the morning?"

He considered me for a moment then answered. "I figured you're not much of a morning person. Sometimes we get lucky when we roust at dawn."

"Lucky? I can think of better ways to get lucky in the morning." I heard snorts of laughter in the squad room and realized what I said. "I mean, I don't think your waking me up at dawn is lucky."

The laughter increased, and Dirk raised one eyebrow.

"I don't mean lucky, lucky, I just mean...crap. Never mind."

"I see I was right about your inability to function before coffee." He turned and called Allen over. "Get us a couple to go from Dora's." He handed Allen a few dollars, stopped and added a fiver. "Better make hers an extra large."

"Gee, big spender."

"Count yourself lucky that you're getting any at all."

Nice. The squad room laughter wasn't at my expense this time.

The teasing light left Dirk's eyes. "Look, let's get to it. I've got a case to crack."

He tossed the evidence bag on the desk. "We found this powder in your home. Any idea how the bag got there?"

I didn't touch the evidence, didn't even prod it with a pencil. "I've never seen it before." I looked at him.

"Where was it found?"

He hesitated. "In the kitchen. Cabinet above the fridge."

"Heck, that's so hard to get at, I use it to store stuff I never use."

"Like crystal champagne flutes?"

I felt heat flush my cheeks. Sure, my love life sucked, which meant it couldn't get worse. See? Proof being I sat surrounded by men. Not by choice, but still.

Maybe I'd been wrong not to call a lawyer or at least Ginger before leaving the house. The evidence, falsified though it was, piled up. Dirk didn't think I was guilty, did he?

Dirk didn't push the line of questioning surrounding my wine glasses. Instead, he shoved the evidence bag holding the papers at me. "Look familiar?"

"Yes. You showed me those earlier. Where were those found?"

"Same place."

"That's pretty cliché, don't you think? Do you really believe I'm that stupid?"

Allen set two coffees on the desk and handed change to Dirk. "I can vouch for Katie. She almost flunked science more than once."

I fumbled the cup. "Thanks, I think."

Dirk relaxed into his chair and sipped coffee. "Really? And now she works an Auto-CAD for a construction company. That's right, isn't it, Ms. Sheridan?"

I closed my eyes, knowing where his questions headed.

"That type of work takes some mathematical

ability, doesn't it?"

"So I'm a late bloomer. Besides, math and science aren't the same thing."

"Really?"

"Not to me. Look, ask me your questions so I can get to work, okay? I'm going to be late as it is. We've got a big job and I don't have time to waste."

Dirk leaned forward, slapping his palm against his desk. I grabbed my coffee cup. "You think a murder investigation is a waste of time?"

"Questioning me is, because I don't know anything." I leaned forward and we were nose to crooked nose. "And by the way, doesn't it take more time than a few days to get lab results? How did you know what to look for and why did you come to me?"

"Preliminary results point to ricin."

Baloney and more baloney, but I knew I wouldn't get answers going head to head with Dirk. Someone with clout pushed the lab or Dirk had good friends there.

"Someone planted that bag and papers at my house. I never saw that stuff before, and I bet you won't find my prints. So ask me your questions, I'll give you my answers, and we'll both be on our way. Unless you want to hand me a phone so I can call a lawyer."

"Fine." Dirk lifted his index finger. "You were within proximity to the deceased before he died of poison found in your home."

He added his middle finger. "You attempted resuscitation, which could have been a cover to introduce the poison."

Another finger joined the rest. "Your best friend is being blackmailed after an affair with the victim."

The final finger rose. "We had a tip." He lowered the accusatory digits. "Sounds like means, motive, and opportunity to me. Settle in. We're going to be here a while."

"A tip?" I'm not everyone's idea of a best friend, but who would accuse me? My brain tried to embrace the inconceivable idea. Only one answer remained possible.

"I'm being framed." My voice sounded weak even to me, and I knew I'd better call a lawyer, pronto. Not that I had money for an attorney. The situation sucked.

"That's one possibility." He sipped again.

My heart pounded, and I couldn't sit still. Fidgeting probably looked bad, but I couldn't help myself. "I don't even know how the poison was administered, so how can I be the killer?"

Dirk's lips turned up at the corners. "Look, I think you're the last person to kill with poison or any other weapon. I don't believe you're a murderer, but my boss isn't so sure."

I blinked. "Why would someone frame me?"

"I'm hoping you can tell me." He tossed his empty cup into the trash and grabbed a pen. "Let's go over Saturday's events. Maybe you've forgotten something important."

I covered my groan with a long sip of coffee. This day sucked already, and the clock hands weren't anywhere close to noon. I capitulated and dredged my brain for answers. Not because Dirk's eyes were so sexy—a retainer would drain my bank account and max out my credit cards.

But the thought I may need an attorney stayed front and center in my consciousness.

Chapter Eight

Allen gave me a ride home in his car, not in a Granville Falls cruiser. I sat looking at my house, too tired to move. My sweet bungalow didn't seem like a refuge anymore. Especially because my internal alarm system sounded loud and clear.

"You guys locked up when you hauled me in to jail, right?"

"When we invited you for questioning, but yeah, we locked everything."

The door wasn't wide open, but didn't look shut tight, either. "So Allen, why is my front door not closed all the way?"

He squinted at my door then phoned for back up. We sat tight until a cruiser showed up followed by Dirk in his unmarked. I stayed in the car while they searched my house for intruders. The all clear sounded and I walked through every room, looking for anything out of place while the patrol guys checked with my neighbors. They were likely all playing Bingo at St. Bartholomew, but I kept my mouth shut. Ya never know.

Dirk leaned against the door, watching me check for missing items. He knew better than me that I should look for stuff added, not taken. My house existed in remodel mode. Anything could have been tucked anywhere. That thought gave me pause, but nobody would chase me from my bungalow.

He pushed away from the wall. "You okay?"

"The Sphinx speaks."

Looking every inch Cop Sexy, he sauntered toward me. "I guess I deserve that, huh?" His hands slid into his back pockets. Lucky hands. "Look, I have a job to do. I really had no choice but to bring you in."

"I get that. I know it looks bad, but I didn't kill Morgan."

"Everyone in the room heard you say you needed to go to the bathroom. If you were trying to be furtive, your ploy didn't work."

Was that a little smile I saw on his lips? Nope, guess not. I got an idea. "My exit from the room gave someone opportunity to kill Morgan if her mat lay close to his. Then she could blame me. I wish I knew who started the rumor that I spoke with Morgan before I left."

"So do I. Morgan had already been dosed when you passed him."

I shivered. "How do you know?"

"We've got the time of death. The ME worked her way backwards. Given the probable poison type, she extrapolated the dose size and gave us a closer time line."

"So you knew I wasn't the killer."

"No, I didn't. Still don't. The timeline doesn't rule you out, because he was poisoned at the start of or during class."

His blunt words shocked me into speechlessness.

Dirk moved closer and smoothed his palm over my hair. His hand was the only warm spot on my body. "We've got an open investigation. Everyone is a suspect."

I wished he wouldn't keep reminding me. My feet moved me away from his soothing touch. Cooperating with the enemy was off my agenda.

"My cop sense says you didn't kill Anderson. I need facts that'll help me find the real killer. You're sure Morgan didn't look sick during class?"

I remained in the suspect pool and jumpsuit orange didn't complement my complexion. Helping him find the killer looked the only way to avoid unflattering photos in the newspapers.

"He might have been a little unsteady at the end, but I wouldn't know. Saturday was my first class."

"Unsteady, how?"

"I don't know exactly. It's a feeling." Ginger would kill me, but she always noticed more than me. "You should ask Ginger. She mentioned his goofy balance the other day."

"Trying to get rid of me?"

"No, I just want to clear my name and get on with my life."

He slid closer and twisted a strand of my hair around his finger. "Does that include bringing your wine glasses out of retirement?"

Heavy footsteps sounded in the hall. "Detective Johnson? You here?"

Dirk dropped my hair and stepped away from me. "Living room."

Allen entered holding a note in an evidence bag. "Detective, I found this inside a coffee mug."

He handed over the bag and gave me a worried look. Great. More crap piled up against me.

Dirk handed the bag back to Allen. "Get that to the lab and tell them we need a priority workup."

I couldn't believe he wouldn't show me what they'd found. "Hey, aren't you going to show me what some dick planted in here?"

"Katie, you don't want to see the note."

"Why not? Is it a photograph of me injecting Morgan?" I shook my head. "Can't be. I hate needles. Okay, then it's a signed confession with my name, saying I killed him. Right?"

When neither man answered I repeated my last question. "Right?"

Dirk motioned to Allen, who remained standing still. "Go."

Allen shot out of my house, leaving Dirk and I alone, at least for the moment. "You don't want to know what the note said."

"Yes, I do. If it concerns me, I damn well do want to know."

He sighed and shook his head. "You have to promise me you won't go off half-cocked with a frying pan."

"Then you'll tell me? Okay, I promise."

He aged in that minute. Watching him was like looking at fast-frame photography, the way his eyes grew sad and his shoulders slumped. Whatever baggage the man carried weighed heavy.

"The note says, 'Your friend now owes a quarter million. Tell the cops and she dies.'"

My vision blurred and my legs collapsed. Lucky I stood in front of the couch. "Who's doing this?"

Dirk knelt on the floor in front of me. "We're gonna find this dirt bag. I promise."

The cops left, and I went through my kitchen trashing anything powdered or lace-able with poison.

There's never much food at my house, but I like to bake. An unopened ten-pound bag of flour went in the garbage along with all my other dry goods. Even my coffee. I love my Arabica beans, but someone broke in twice. I wouldn't take chances.

Dirk asked for a police patrol and guard on the house. I figured the effort was too little too late, but the attention gave me some comfort.

Jim called to check on me, too. He told me to take the rest of the week off. I had an idea of how to spend the next day, but then I'd need to get back to the Auto-CAD. Jim would screw my machine up for sure.

One more thing was certain. I needed answers. I'm no cop, but I'd lived in Granville Falls all my life. Ginger was the only person I trusted, but I still knew how to get the dirt. If Ginger couldn't help, Mona would. With no coffee in the house, I'd have to stop at the Chocolate Fix in the morning.

Chocolate and coffee for breakfast. A hardship, but I'd struggle through.

****

Mona, Ginger and I sat at one of the Chocolate Fix's tables, inhaling mochas and chocolate croissants. The combo rocks out and our inattention was a travesty. We didn't savor our treats. Nerves have that affect on people.

Ginger licked her fingers. "So when I thought back, I realized Morgan's last pose wasn't strong, and he had us in the Savasana earlier than usual. He almost sank onto his mat. That wasn't like him."

Mona swallowed her coffee. "Dang, I always hated the corpse pose. Achieving total relaxation while laying on a one-inch piece of foam covering a hard floor? Not in my lifetime."

I bit into the pastry. Sheer heaven. "Dirk said Morgan was poisoned that morning."

Ginger looked startled. "I guess he must have been, but how could that be possible?"

Mona sat like a statue. "Can you tell me how he was killed?" Her face looked pasty and she didn't appear to breathe.

"I guess so. I mean, the information hasn't hit the papers, so you may want to keep this to yourself, but Dirk said ricin is suspected."

The chocolatier's eyes narrowed. "Ricin? The same stuff someone sent in a letter to the White House last spring? I recall another news story last year. A death in the Midwest, or maybe a nut job threatening people." She leaned her chin on the palm of her hand. "Some assassin used ricin to kill a Russian or maybe a Bulgarian bigwig. Made all the papers. I think the story got made into a film. I don't remember for sure. Humph. Ricin."

"Do you know how the poison works?" I held my breath waiting for her answer.

"I'm pretty sure the substance is most deadly ingested or inhaled. I suppose ricin could be injected. I do know the amount needed to kill someone is small." She tilted her head to the side. "Usually it takes a day or so before death. Guess someone gave him enough to make sure he'd bite the big one sooner than later. Or maybe he had a bad heart." She snorted. "Not that he had one."

I watched Mona's finger tap-tap the marble. Suddenly I was noticing tells and playing detective too. It wouldn't take a psychologist to pick up on her nervousness.

"Mona, do the cops know about your friend? The one who bought Morgan the expensive watch?"

She stiffened. "No, and I'm not giving her over."

"I get that. I'm hoping she'll talk with the cops on her own."

Mona's intense glare reminded me of Dirk. "Why would she do something that stupid?"

Ginger leaned forward. "Because if she volunteers, the police may stop looking at her as a suspect. That's what Detective Johnson told me when I spoke with him yesterday. He promised me anonymity if possible."

Mona's finger stopped tapping. She stared at Ginger. "You? I never would have believed you hooked up with Yoga Man."

My friend gave a sick laugh. "Me, either. Morgan got so intense at the end. He even asked me to get a divorce so we could elope. I almost believed him."

I felt my forehead crinkle. I knew Ginger wouldn't make up the story, but eloping with Morgan? According to rumor, that wasn't his style. He was strictly love 'em and leave 'em. Or rather, screw 'em and blackmail 'em. 'Course, Ginger's sweet, loaded and gorgeous—everyone says so, not just me. Maybe Morgan looked to Ginger for the big score.

Something about the intimidation continued to bother me. Why did Morgan hint for gifts, then turn around and send notes with photos? The notes weren't signed, the messages used cut out letters. We assumed Morgan blackmailed the women after he dumped them, but maybe he wasn't the extortionist. Could be someone else pursued the blackmail making Morgan as much a victim as the women.

And what if a husband learned about the affair his wife had and wanted revenge? Wouldn't that be a motive for murder?

Ginger cleared her throat. "I told Rob about Morgan."

Yikes. "But did he know while Morgan was alive?"

She didn't answer for a minute. Mona left to make us another round of mocha.

Ginger spoke quickly in a soft voice. "Rob didn't seem surprised when I told him. I thought he'd be upset, but he just had that stern jawed look, you know the one."

I nodded. The grim look. If Rob were British he'd have a permanent stiff upper lip. "So you think he already knew about your affair with Morgan."

Tears welled in my friend's eyes. "Yes," she whispered.

"Sweetie, is Rob having an affair?"

"I don't know. He says not, but—"

I read more than I wanted to in her trailed off sentence. Could Rob have killed Morgan? Had he really played golf on Saturday morning? Did either of us want to know for sure?

Mona came back with the fresh mocha and a plate of truffles. She sat and let out a sigh. "I'm calling my friend and letting her know Detective Johnson may want to hear her story."

Holding down a cheer, I managed a quiet thank you.

"I can't promise anything for her, but I think she'll understand why she has to talk with the cops. Damn men cause more trouble than they're worth." She wiped her hand over her eyes. "You said Johnson promised he'd keep her involvement quiet if he could?"

Ginger put her hand over Mona's and squeezed. "I think he'll do what he can to protect the women in this case." She patted my hand. "All of them."

Mona eyed me up and down. "Got yourself a hot one, huh? Good for you." She stood. "I've gotta open in fifteen minutes, so you can either give me a hand or move it."

We gave her a hand.

****

"Can you come to the impound lot? We found Morgan's abandoned SUV. We want to know if it's the same one involved in your hit and run on Sunday."

Dirk's deep voice reverberated in parts of me that never see the light of day. I about fanned myself, until I realized what he'd asked.

"Hello to you, too, and where's the impound lot?"

He gave me directions even though I already knew the lot he meant. Granville Falls had become a bedroom community for Charlotte, but the town remained fairly small. The chill bumps his voice created on my spine weren't small, though. Not at all.

I had my own car back and arrived at the lot in record time. My legs shook when I got out and stood looking at an SUV that may or may not have been the one that almost hit me. Dirk and Matt joined me.

Dirk gestured to the SUV. "That the one?"

"I don't know for sure. Can we get closer?"

Matt unlocked the compound. "Have you seen this SUV before?"

I walked closer. "This was Morgan's? Talk is he loved to advertise. Why isn't there a sign on his door promoting the studio?"

Matt looked at his partner. Dirk rubbed his forehead with two fingers. "The SUV is Morgan's. The door sign is magnetic, and whoever stole the vehicle removed it."

"When was it stolen?"

Matt punched Dirk in the upper arm. "Hey, she knows the right questions, maybe you should partner up with her."

Dirk's answering glare had Matt clearing his throat before he continued. "The assistant couldn't nail down a time or date. A patrol found the SUV abandoned, no prints."

I circled the vehicle again. "Guys, this looks like the same one. It has tinted windows and the grill is the same. I didn't see the rear bumper because I landed ass over teakettle. Have you asked Mrs. Haywood?"

Matt answered. "We don't need to now that you've seen the vehicle." Why did Dirk remain silent?

"So I can go?"

Dirk put a hand on my arm. "In a minute. I have a question or two for you." He jerked his head to the side and Matt stepped away. "What have you been up to? Do you think this investigation is a game?"

I said the first thing that came to mind. "Huh?" My articulation knows no bounds.

"Look, I don't want you getting hurt. Several women have come forward to report blackmail notes received after their affairs with Morgan. They said you asked them to speak up."

"Me? I asked a friend of a friend, that's all."

"Well stop asking friends of friends, okay?" His hand tightened. "There's a freaking murderer loose."

"Yeah, and he or she is determined to lay the

murder on me." I pulled my arm away. "I have the right to defend myself, and if that means asking questions, so be it."

"Defending yourself and looking for a killer are two different things. A second grader could break into your house."

"I've got deadbolts, remember?"

"What you need is another place to stay until we get this guy."

"I thought you were looking for a woman. Isn't poison a woman's weapon?"

He hesitated. I saw it cost him to give me any information at all. "In this case, either a man or woman could be the perp."

Rob's face flashed in my brain and I pushed him out before my expression gave Dirk something to think about. "I hate to say this, but a woman seems to have more motive."

"Unless a jealous husband took him out."

I closed my eyes against the returning image of Rob.

Dirk's growl lifted my lids in a hurry. "What do you know?"

"Nothing." My cuticles claimed my attention. "How could the killer know how to get the ricin? I mean, poison isn't a subject taught in school. Unless the school is Hogwarts."

"You can find anything on the Internet."

I snapped my fingers and Dirk rolled his eyes in response, as if he knew what I'd say next. He probably did, given his intelligence factor.

"Have you checked the Internet and tried to match up those instructions you found in my house with say,

Wikipedia? Hey and then you can check browser histories."

"We'd need a warrant and probable cause, but yeah, we figured that out."

My fallen expression must have jogged something in Dirk's cop heart because he squeezed my shoulder. "Thanks for the ideas."

Then he gave me a small shake. "But stop asking questions. You're not a trained detective, and the killer is getting desperate. Don't let yourself get thrown under the wheels, okay?"

His earnest gaze urged me to pay attention. Too bad I don't follow directions well. "You may want to talk with Brandi Wells. I heard she was one of Morgan's flings, and she wasn't happy when he dumped her."

His face darkened. I knew he knew I wouldn't make promises.

"Better take Matt with you. I hear Flash is looking for a new boyfriend."

A smirk crossed Dirk's face. "Jealous?"

"Nah, I don't want to break in a new detective if Flash sinks her fangs and drains your blood."

I ignored Dirk's scowl, enjoying Matt's laughter as I walked to my car. The police were looking at men too. That added another twist and put Ginger back in their sites via Rob. I hoped to heaven his alibi checked out.

Chapter Nine

Ginger licked sugar from her fingers. "So did your sexy cop ask you out?

"No." I blurted out my newest worry. "He said they think the murderer could be a man."

She stopped moving, with a truffle just millimeters from her mouth. What control. "Why a man?"

"I don't know, but... do you think Rob could be involved?"

"Rob?" Ginger snorted and replaced the truffle on her plate. "What makes you think he'd get his hands dirty?"

Whoa. If Ginger's magenta colored face wasn't enough clue, her clipped tone told me she nursed a big mad. "How bad is it?"

"My marriage?"

My expression conveyed my worry. She answered without me saying a word.

"I'm not in a marriage anymore. Seems more like the hotel business."

She raised her head, frowning. "He's not here much, and when he is, I feel like I'm talking with a stranger. I can't tell you the last time we made love. So I make sure he has food to eat, clean towels and plenty of shampoo."

The reason for her fling with Morgan rang crystal clear, and I wanted to slap Rob upside the head. Ginger might have cheated, but in my mind, Rob pushed her into an affair.

I gulped, uneasy about asking for more detail, even from my best friend. Hurting her remained the last thing I wanted to do. "Do you think he's having an affair?"

"At first I thought not, but now I'm not so sure."

"Why is that?"

She examined her manicure. "Rob's always been easily distracted, and I thought he was busy at work. He was in charge of that big merger, you know."

I knew. The merger completed months ago.

"Then after the merger, he started working harder, longer hours. No explanation when I asked, just that I shouldn't worry." She poured tea into our cups and picked up another truffle, only to put it back. "Then I decided to get out of the house. I thought exercise would help and that's when I started yoga lessons."

And we both knew what happened after that. Morgan.

"Do you think Rob knew about you and Morgan before you told him?"

"At first I thought not." Ginger flexed her fingers. "Now I'm not so sure. Rob's been, oh, I guess you could say smug."

Shivers ran down my spine. That didn't sound good.

"You don't think Rob—" I couldn't finish the question.

"I don't know what to think."

My gaze ran around the kitchen. "But he's still gone all the time. Does he even care?"

Ginger shook her head no. "I don't know. I truly don't."

Damn, I had to ask the next question and wished it could go unvoiced. "Does he love you enough to kill for you?"

"Katie, the Rob I married was kind, thoughtful, generous. I'd never cheat on that Rob. But I'm not living with the man I married. Not anymore."

That was so not what I wanted to hear.

"Ginger, do you know where Rob was last Saturday?"

She half laughed. "I don't know where he is right now." She chewed on her thumb. "He said he was in Charlotte with customers. Golfing."

Golfing would be easy to check, if he came down to needing an alibi.

"Sometimes I think all we have left is divorce. But, Katie, I really hope not. Shame on me, but I still love the man."

We sat quietly and drank our tea. Ginger still wasn't cleared by the police. She hadn't mentioned Rob's temper. His anger didn't show often, but when it did, his outbursts were legendary. Rob may have treated Ginger with kindness, but he also had a protective streak bordering on possessive. A former varsity athlete, Rob could easily have threatened Morgan. But murder? Who knew what would push someone over the edge?

When I finally stood to leave, neither of us felt better, and I couldn't blame the stone cold tea in my mug. One way or another, Ginger faced a screwed-up marriage and I had difficulty moving away from a potential murder tag. We hugged.

Ginger whispered, "Please don't tell Detective Johnson about Rob. He can't have killed Morgan. The capacity for murder is just not in him."

My inner cynic deferred but I agreed to keep our inferences secret. Any involvement Rob had would come out, sure as shit.

****

Dirk sat in his car outside my house when I returned. He unfolded his length from the front seat and sauntered across my lawn. I could have stood next to my car watching his display of masculine grace all day. Too bad he spoiled the picture with a scolding.

"Why don't you have a porch light burning?"

"Why don't you mind your own business?"

"You are my business."

Well, that unexploded bomb sat between us for a minute while I tried to gather my thoughts. "Excuse me?"

"To serve and protect. That's what I do."

Uh huh. I believed that because anything more would be way too much for my brain.

"Okay, Mr. Serve and Protect. My porch light burned out last night. I meant to change the bulb, but I forgot."

"Get a bulb. I'll change it right now."

The serve and protect business gave me hives, but, jumpy from the break-ins, his company felt pretty good. We entered the house, which had been locked, thank you, and I got the bulb and a stepstool. A couple of longnecks cooled in the fridge, so I pulled one out for him, just in case he got thirsty after the strenuous work of changing a bulb. I poured myself a glass of wine, arranged some cheese on a plate and pulled out the crackers. Mama taught me to make nice with men who could do household chores.

Dirk put the old bulb on the counter and pointed to the beer. "Mine?"

"Yep." Crap. Now we're speaking in couple's shorthand. What the?

"So, Detective Johnson, why are you here? Can't be for my stellar cooking skills."

"Mind if I sit?" I pointed to the chair and he settled in. "I need to ask you again about Saturday."

My head throbbed, right behind my eyes. The story had been repeated so often I doubted there could be anything new to add. I sighed. "Okay."

"We've narrowed down the murder weapon."

My spine straightened as if someone pulled me up by the head. "Really? What was it?"

"I can't really say, but I need you to think back to the victim's actions during class."

I'd get the weapon information out of him or my name wasn't Katie Sheridan. "I'll tell you again what I saw if you tell me how he died."

Dirk sighed. "Okay, look. I'll give you our working hypothesis, but you can't tell anyone. Not your best friend or even your cat."

He knew I had no cat, so he meant Ginger. His expression told me he wouldn't back down, so if I wanted the information, I had no choice.

"I promise."

Dirk carefully matched cheese and a cracker. He took a bite, chewed and swallowed. I about crawled out of my skin, but I knew he stalled for effect.

"The man's yoga mat and some strange foam blocks held enough ricin to kill three people. Maybe more. How long did he handle the mat or the block during class?"

I knew his thoughts were off base before he finished the question. "He didn't."

"What you mean he didn't use either one?"

"No, not until the end of the class. Morgan wasn't on his mat like the rest of us. He walked around the room, correcting poses for most of the students." I paused, reviewing the scene in my head. "When he demonstrated poses, he didn't use the mat at the front. He just went into the pose from wherever he was at the time."

"Is that usual?"

"Got me. My first class, remember?"

Taking a gulp of wine, I spent more time in review. "Morgan didn't return to his mat until right before we went into the corpse pose."

Dirk did a great second look. "The what?"

"I know. Creepy, isn't it? That's what the last pose is called. You lay flat out on your back. Laying flat is supposed to induce total relaxation, but it didn't work for me."

His lips curved up at the corners then dropped down. "So Anderson didn't use the mat until the end of the class." He tapped his fingers against his lips. Lucky fingers. "Did you notice anyone near his mat? Either before or during class?"

I searched my brain cells, but nothing came to mind. "Nope, can't say that I did."

"Can you tell me who was positioned adjacent to the victim?"

"Flash was directly in front and to his left. You'll have to ask her who the others were. I didn't notice."

He made a note then tapped his pen against the page. "The blocks. Were they used in class?"

The question differed from the ones repeated ad naseum on Saturday, so I thought for a moment. "Morgan didn't need them, I guess. A few people used blocks, but I didn't see who did or didn't."

"And everyone brings their own mats, is that right?"

"Everyone who has one. The studio provides mats for beginners like me."

"That helps quite a bit. Thanks." He moved to stand.

"Whoa. Where do you think you're going?"

He grabbed another cheese and cracker combo. "Thanks for the beer and snacks, but I gotta get back to the office."

"That's all? You give me one crumb of information, drink my beer, eat my snacks and leave?"

I waited while he finished chewing. "Oh, sorry. I should say thanks for the lead. Thanks. Gotta go."

I rose and moved to block the doorway. "Nyuh uh. Are you saying Morgan may not have been the intended victim?"

"Nope. That was his mat. His assistant gave us a positive ID."

"So Morgan *was* the intended victim all along."

Dirk raised one eyebrow.

"You can't even tell me that? Give me a break. I mean, you're not telling me how the ricin was used. Or if any of the women he screwed had a reason to kill him. Or how big of a bank account he had. Or who inherits, for cripes sake."

He moved closer. "I can tell you one thing."

Our gazes collided. "What's that?"

"This." He palmed my cheeks, tilted my head and

laid on a kiss so hot my brain exploded. Not really, but it sure felt that way. Not only did my brain become mush, time stopped.

One of his hands moved to cradle the back of my head, the other stroked my cheek. I could taste the beer on his exploring tongue, and his chest was hard against mine. My hands moved up to his shoulders, then my greedy fingers reached for his hair. Yep, those badly cut, dark, silky-smooth and tangle free strands. Smooth until I had my wicked way.

Dirk lifted his mouth from mine but his lips and tongue came back for another taste. I sucked that movable organ like there was no tomorrow. From Dirk's moans, I'd say we both hit the jackpot.

He had more discipline than me, because he pulled away, sucking my bottom lip as he left. I licked my lip after him and he looked ready to dive back in. His darkened eyes held promise, but Dirk shifted me from the doorway. He moved around me and down the hall.

My sluggish brain couldn't think of a way to stop him so I could get more answers about Morgan's death. Huh. The jerk manipulated me with a kiss. Not that I'm complaining, but still. His payback would be hell.

"Forget your questions about the murder and let me handle the case. Lock the damn door. And keep the porch light on all night."

So much for tender sentiments from Mr. Protect and Serve.

****

The alarm rang good news, bad news. Good news because I was still alive, bad news because I didn't feel like working on design plans. But Jim's a great boss and he'd be lost without me.

Early morning was still dark and the kitchen lights glared at my tired eyes. No coffee brewed automatically because I forgot to buy the beans, and caffeine-free wasn't the way I liked to start the day. Somehow I kicked my butt into gear and headed into the office.

Jim looked up when I entered. "What the hell are you doing here? I told you to stay home."

"Good morning, Jim. So good to be back." I waited for him to catch my drift but he didn't pick up. Someday I've gotta figure out why my favorite men have no social skills. "I can't let you mess up the project plans for much longer. You'll go broke in a week."

"You puppy. I been at this longer than you've been alive."

"That doesn't mean you know the Auto-CAD." I pointed at the stacks of paper covering his desk. "Or that you're organized."

He rubbed his brush cut a few times and gave a low grunt. "All right, I could use your help."

Construction Speak Translation: he was glad to have me back.

Jim ducked out of the trailer to avoid my wrath. Papers tilted in haphazard piles over most of the desk surface. Styrofoam cups took up the slack, perched precariously, waiting to dump their cold contents over plans I recognized as originals. My boss knew I hated a messy workspace and didn't want to hear my bitching. Especially when he caused the disarray.

The coffee perked hot and handy, and my mug got filled before I tackled the pile of work in front of me. Concentration wasn't easy knowing my best friend faced blackmail, someone used my house like a bus station locker, and a hot cop was, well, hot for me. At least his interest seemed that way.

I needed to think about life, not death. Jim returned with one of his supervisors, but neither said a word. He just pretended my presence meant business as usual. And that's what made him a kick-ass boss. Maybe polite social skills are overrated.

Lunch came and went before I got the updated plans organized and ready for each job we worked. I liked feeling in control for a change.

My muscles were tight from sitting all morning and my stomach growled. I needed a stretch and some food and knew where to get both. A quick fifteen-minute walk later, Dora's came into view.

I entered and wanted to turn around and leave. Seated with heads close together were Flash and Dirk. Flash had her hands moving along Dirk's arm, and he didn't look too sad about her caresses. My appetite disappeared but my chance of leaving passed. Flash's smirk and loud greeting told me I'd been made.

"Well, there she is now, Miss Lifesaver. Practiced any CPR lately?" She kept her hold on Dirk's arm. "Detective Johnson asked me to lunch. Wasn't that sweet of him?" She, honest-to-God, batted her eyelashes at him.

I had to swallow my automatic retort and a mouthful of bile before answering. "Sweet, Flash? Yes, I can see where you'd think that."

Dirk shot me an apologetic look. My palms itched to slap it off his face, but I played nice. "I'll just leave you to your lunch. Enjoy the food."

The statement was silly because their empty plates told me they'd finished eating before I walked in. Maybe they'd been planning on afternoon delight for dessert prior to my interruption.

I walked my misery to a stool at the counter. Dora raised her eyebrows and I nodded. Less than a minute later, she set a large glass of iced tea in front of me.

The café owner leaned toward me as she handed me a straw. "Now that's a bee with an itch."

I gathered my courage and glanced into the mirror behind the counter. The scene was not reassuring. Flash had scooted closer to Dirk. She leaned so close she could have been his napkin. Their contrasting coloring looked good together, like a fancy salt and pepper set.

"Why do you say that, Dora? You gotta admit, the man is hot. You'd be in Flash's place if you thought you could get away with it." So would I, even if saying so made me want to cry. Why I'd ever think Cop Sexy could be interested in me?

"She walked in here like she had a right to order me around."

Oops. That would've gone over well. Not. Even knowing Flash had made Dora's "B" list didn't cheer me.

Dora squinted. "Sweetie, don't put your arm down there. I missed a spot."

Too late.

My forearm slid across the counter. I jerked forward and came close to dumping my glass. A look at my arm told the story. Smeared ketchup from elbow to wrist. I swiveled off the stool and headed for the ladies.

Focused on washing off the gunk I didn't look up when another customer walked in.

"Little Miss Murderer. I thought you were arrested, but here you are, walking around free. I'm glad I have a big, strong policeman to protect me."

Gag me. "Get over yourself, Brandi. It's not my fault Morgan dumped you." I stared at her reflection in the mirror. "And, unlike you, I don't put the make on anything with a penis, so stop spreading the stories I ran after Morgan. I didn't know the man."

Her ugly smile told me her next words would match the look. "Then why did you make sure no one else could get close when you jumped his bones?"

"Oh, for cripes sake." Tossing the messy paper towel into the sink, I turned to face her. "I did CPR. Not the most romantic setting for a seduction in case you don't know. Not that I'd have anything to do with a man who screwed you." I put a finger on my cheek and tilted my head in my best coquette move. "Oh, wait. He screwed you, then screwed you over, didn't he? My mistake."

Flash pointed her index finger at me. "I'll thank you to mind your own business."

I couldn't believe someone actually used that phrase in real life, but she did. "Brandi, stop your story-telling or I'll slap your ass with a defamation suit so hard and fast you won't be able to sit for a month."

Flash's face could have doubled for a stoplight. "I heard about your moves from a reliable source. You'll have to prove you didn't kill Morgan." She pivoted and huffed to the door. Whirling, she added misery to insult. "Stay away from the cop. I deserve a guy like Dirk. You wouldn't know what to do with him."

The mirror reflected her momentary yearning expression. Flash was vulnerable? Like a snake.

My stomach churned and I couldn't hide out in the ladies all afternoon. I pulled half a dozen hand towels from the dispenser and scrubbed my arm dry.

Avoiding looking at Dirk's table, I moved toward the counter.

The hunger pangs were gone, but even if they weren't, Flash's presence would ruin any food Dora could serve. Not to mention Dirk, the traitor. Kissing me like the earth moved then cozying up with the skank. Over him, over him, over him.

My unresisting hormones woke up when Dirk slid onto the stool next to mine. I ignored them and him.

"Why do you call her Flash?"

I let him wait for an answer. "Because she's a flash in the pan." My gaze met his over my coffee cup. "Kind of like certain cops I almost know."

My modus operandi didn't include feeling jealous anger over a man. Especially a man I didn't really know. One who could arrest me at any moment. My hormones didn't listen to my rationalizations. They wanted to get down and dirty, the sooner the better. I really needed to get a life.

"Look, I have to follow every lead."

"Really? Flash's lead is to the bedroom. You gonna follow her there, too?"

He grinned, the schmuck. "You're cute when you're jealous."

"You and Flash have something in common."

"What's that?"

"You both need to get over yourselves." I let the silence linger. Why did she harp on me as the murderer? And who was her reliable source? I felt like a target decorated my chest.

Dirk's eyes narrowed. "I wonder the same thing. Someone is working hard to throw attention on you."

Crap. I really had to learn not to speak my thoughts

aloud.

Dirk looked ready to comment when Matt walked in. They exchanged cop looks. "Gotta run."

I dug for a ringing cell phone and didn't look up. He put his hand on my arm just as the phone stopped ringing. Our gazes tangled.

"Flash is just a source. You're more than that."

"Oh, really? Like a major suspect? Or just a material witness?"

His look incinerated me without him using a match. "I'll call."

Dirk left the cafe and my hungry gaze followed him while my heart did a Sound of Music imitation. The cafe owner walked over with a new glass of iced tea.

"Dora, I think I'll have a burger after all. Make that a platter."

I knew from her smile she wanted to comment on Dirk and my renewed appetite when my phone rang again. Ginger. The connection was barely made when she dropped her bomb.

"I just received another note."

Dora stood close. I figured she could hear Ginger. "Forget the burger, just load me up with an extra large tea to go." The café owner walked away with a frown.

"Sweetie, calm down." I lowered my voice. "What does it say?"

"It's instructions on delivering the money."

"I'll be right over."

Chapter Ten

"If I notify the police, Rob's life is in danger."

Ginger recounted the note's main point, ignoring the fact that I held it in my hand. She nibbled her cuticle.

The blackmailer had it in for Ginger, no doubt. Why? And how could we handle this pay-off without getting killed?

Even though I'd read the note, I didn't have the sentences memorized like Ginger so I re-read every word. Block printing filled in portions of the demand. Guess the jerk-wad couldn't find all the words he needed already in print.

Pack $250,000 in small bills into a bright red duffle bag. Go to Graceland Cemetery on Poplar Tent Road tomorrow night. At exactly 1:45 am leave the bag on the Augusta Caulfield gravesite. No dye packs. No police. Mess with me and your husband dies.

"Who the hell is Augusta Caulfield?" Ginger didn't answer. "Never mind, her grave is probably located in the deepest, darkest part of the cemetery. The jerk couldn't make this easy, like, 'leave a knapsack marked John Smith at the Kannapolis train station's lost and found counter.' No, we have to get wired on coffee and nerves to show up in the dead of night. Dead of night. In the cemetery. Geez, I'm giving myself chill bumps."

Ginger answered with a dull tone. "You aren't

going with me."

"Baloney. I'll hide in the backseat if I have to. You aren't going there alone. End of discussion."

She grabbed my hand in a vice-like grip. "I can't risk your life or Rob's."

I wanted to remind her Rob treated her like a hotel maid, but I kept quiet. My friend loved a man who made a Polar Bear look warm and fuzzy. All I could do was stand by her. And ride shotgun to the drop off. That wasn't optional.

"Have you thought about how you'll get that kind of cash together overnight?"

She nodded. "Ben Winchester at the bank owes me a favor. I alerted him when you told me about the note Detective Johnson confiscated, and he's got the bills ready. I'll get the money in the morning."

"You're not going alone. I don't want this guy to pull a switch and hit you over the head when you come out of the bank."

Ginger smiled, the first happy expression I'd seen on her face in too long. "Ben is delivering the cash here, so stop worrying."

"What time?"

"What?"

"When is the money delivery? I've never seen that much cash in one place. I thought I'd play with it before you hand it over."

She gave me the rolled eye I deserved. "Be here at noon. We'll have salad."

****

I showed at noon, but the lettuce Ginger had waiting didn't feature Ben Franklin's face. A substantial-sized metal suitcase stood next to the table,

106

and my hands itched to open the case, just for a look at a quarter mil in small bills. I lifted the suitcase, surprised at the weight.

"Geez, I didn't know cash could be so heavy." I shut my mouth and mentally kicked myself. Worry weighed heavier than the cash with a life on the line.

"What's this about cash?" Rob walked in. Based on Ginger's reaction, she didn't expect him for lunch. His glance took in the metal suitcase then moved to Ginger.

"Oh, I was just saying I need to get some cash for our shopping trip." I prayed that'd fly.

He pointed to the suitcase resting at my feet. "Going somewhere?"

"What? Oh, no, um, that's some equipment for work. It, um, has a special battery and I didn't think it should stay in the car. You know, because it could get overheated and burn out." Sheesh. That sounded iffy even to me.

"Oh, right." He focused on the case a bit too long then turned to Ginger. "Got something ready for lunch?"

I went into a slow burn. The guy came home unannounced and expected immediate lunch? I'd known Rob longer than the six years he and Ginger had been married, and couldn't believe his actions. His blond haired, blue-eyed All-American good looks hid the devil, plain and simple.

"I've got a salad ready, if you don't mind sharing. Otherwise I can make you a sandwich or heat up last night's pot roast, or—"

"Never mind." Rob's gruff interruption surprised me. "I don't have much time. The salad will have to do." He sat at the place Ginger had set for herself and picked up a fork. "We have any Ranch dressing?"

Ginger found some in the fridge and sat at the table.

"You're not eating?" When she shrugged, he placed a big helping in his bowl. "More for me, then."

Not looking at me, he ate like a pig denied the trough for a week. If he didn't start treating Ginger better, he wouldn't have a week more. I'd see to it myself. Shoot. That wasn't the best thought to entertain, but I promised Ginger I'd have her back. I kept my promises even versus a man I'd considered a friend for years.

Not that the evil entity sitting at the table was the Rob I knew and used to love. I hadn't seen him lately. The ill-tempered and rude man with salad dressing on his chin seemed the exact opposite of the man Ginger married. Either he was stressed to the max or he'd turned into a self-absorbed a-hole. I wouldn't give odds for choice number one.

Could this Rob murder someone? I scrutinized his face while he ate. He had new wrinkles and deep frown lines in his forehead. His athlete's body had turned a tad flabby and there were silver streaks at his temples. Clearly, the man wasn't happy. Could stress lead to murder? He looked at me as if he could tell I weighed his behavior and found him lacking. I glimpsed an expression of deep-seated pain that disappeared faster than I could comprehend the look.

I ducked my head and picked at my salad. Somehow I couldn't see Rob as a murderer, not even if he or his family were threatened. Maybe if he was pinned to the wall, yeah.

His attention rested on the metal case and a

thoughtful expression flitted across his face. Blackmail? That actually seemed likely, and a chill ran down my spine. Maybe Rob schemed with someone else, the real killer. Did he want to leave Ginger and needed a chunk of change to finance his new life? Crap. Ginger would be devastated.

The greens on my plate now resembled compost. I put down my fork and gulped iced tea, but even God's Gift to the South didn't relieve a sandy dry throat. Clearly the marriage floundered, and I couldn't help feeling I had dropped the ball along the way. Friends don't let friends lose husbands they want to keep.

****

We were on our way to the Graceland Cemetery shortly after midnight. I hoped we didn't see Elvis.

Graceland abutted I-85. The main cemetery gates were locked at dusk, but being natives, we knew a side way in. We parked to the side of an interstate entrance ramp. The unofficial turnoff used by truckers for quick snooze time seemed a perfect place to stash the car.

We emerged from Ginger's vehicle to the accompaniment of tree frogs, crickets and late night traffic. We let our eyes acclimate to the available light and then pushed into the brush blocking the dearly departed's view of the interstate. A soft mist swirled through the trees. An owl hooted, a mouse squeaked, and the sound of wings told me a raptor had snagged takeout grub for the kids. Hollywood couldn't have done a better job setting a scary scene, and we hadn't even reached the cemetery proper.

Leaves, still heavy with raindrops from an evening shower, slapped us as we moved closer to our target. I stumbled over exposed roots. "Damn it. Who put that root there?"

"The same person who wanted you to alert anyone in a one-mile radius that you're here."

Ginger's steadying grasp kept me from tripping a second time. We could see a clearing ahead, but the partial moonlight didn't provide much illumination. Wet from the foliage, sticky with humidity and not at all partial to the meeting place, my good humor disintegrated. Two more stumbles and a wet bush later, we hunkered at the wood's edge.

We'd come over earlier and located Miss Caulfield's grave by checking with the cemetery office. The place looked different in the daylight. Now the harmless artificial flower arrangements scattered across the rolling lawns looked menacing—demonic silk bouquets poised to trip the unwary and drag a human-sized meal underground. Clouds moved in and hid the moon.

I pulled my lightweight jacket closer and turned on my superhero flashlight. The batteries were weak and the yellow circle of light burned faint. The tool didn't throw back the dark the way a caped crusader light should. Ginger turned on her pinpoint mag light, helping but not resolving the problem.

"Do you remember how to get to Miss Caulfield's grave?"

Ginger's voice shook. "She should be three rows down from the angel statue."

We started off, and even though Ginger moved no more than two feet from me, I couldn't see her behind the circle of light.

The small cemetery seemed gigantic in the dark. We walked toward the angel monument, just down from the veteran's memorial and catty-corner from the bell tower. The taller statue and structures should have been easy to find, but the century old oaks effectively cloaked everything. I heard a soft exhalation and turned, still moving. Ginger walked close and seemed uninjured, but I stumbled into the cypress hedge. My clumsiness had an element of good luck because the hedge pointed toward the veteran's memorial.

We worked our way to the end and clicked off our flashlights. Our eyes grew accustomed to the filtered light. There was no movement, no night bird flight, no Elvis. I adjusted the heavy duffle bag I had strapped to my back, and inched out of cover.

Graceland Cemetery consisted of an odd hybrid of modest weather-beaten memorial stones, eerie crypts and bronze markers settled into the ground. My feet were completely wet when we found the designated grave. I shifted from one foot to another. Shaking my shoes didn't work. They were soaked and staying that way.

Miss Caulfield was interred in a section of low gravestones surrounded by flat bronze markers. I felt uncomfortable, almost targeted, in an area with very little cover.

Ginger played her light over the gravestone.

Augusta Caulfield

1900-1999

She Keeps Company With Angels

The stone was pretty, with wings feathering her name. Someone had extended the angel theme by centering a small plastic celestial messenger on the memorial stone. Dang. She'd died just short of the century mark. Miss Caulfield would turn in her casket if she knew her grave had become the site of criminal activity. I hoped the angels didn't clue her in. And I hoped we didn't have the chance to speak with Augusta for a good many years.

Three gravesites over, the Rose of Sharon bushes rustled. Ginger and I exchanged glances. Fearful grimaces probably described our expressions best, not that we used a mirror to check. Neither of us wanted to know what animal caused the rustling. Ginger flashed the light on her watch. One-thirty five. Almost show time.

My wet feet signaled my bladder to find a bathroom. "Ginger, I gotta pee."

"I told you not the drink that last cappuccino. You know, if you drank fewer liquids, you wouldn't have to remember where all the bathrooms are everywhere we go. You'll have to hold it. It's not time to leave the bag."

I jiggled in place. The flashlight reflected my movements; a sick yellow glow bounced off the surrounding gravestones. "I'm not kidding. I've really got to go."

Ginger checked her watch. "The note said to leave the bag at exactly one forty-five. That's four more minutes. Before you ask, no, I'm not going to cheat. Can't you hold it?"

"I'm not sure."

"Use a bush then."

I scoped out the dark shadows. "I can wait a few minutes."

My jiggle increased in frequency and my superhero flashlight dropped to the ground, sending a winged signal to Miss Caulfield. I bent to retrieve my light when a whining ping came from the Rose of Sharon's direction. I heard a zinging sound next to my ear.

"Ginger, get down!" She'd already flattened on top of Miss Caulfield when another ping sounded. A piece of the grave marker hit my cheekbone.

Miss Caulfield's angels were gonna be pissed.

We were pinned down. And me without my Superhero's bolo. I reviewed my sins, hoping God would take pity on me and let me in to heaven so I could apologize to Miss Caulfield. Six more shots pinged in quick succession. The shots stopped. I hoped the shooter had left and wasn't reloading. Just in case, I figured I need to make amends.

"Ginger."

"What?"

"I'm sorry for getting you in trouble with Mrs. Crankshaw in third grade."

"Katie? What are you talking about?"

"That we may not get out of here and I want to make it into heaven so I can hang with you. I think my chances are iffy unless I confess."

She didn't answer.

"Ginger?"

"Shh, listen. It sounds like someone is running away."

"Leaving the money behind? That doesn't make sense. He has us trapped."

We both stopped speaking. Sure enough, rustling and muffled swearing were audible moving in a direction away from us. A quick crawl had us meeting in heartfelt hugs.

I retrieved my flashlight, whose batteries were now fit for the surroundings. We struggled to our feet and a barrage of lights hit us square in the eyes.

"Granville Police. Drop your weapons and raise your hands."

Crap. I knew that voice. A silhouetted figure drew closer and I squinted into the light. I knew that swagger too.

"You ladies want to tell me what you're doing out here?"

I shaded my eyes with my hands. "Working the graveyard shift, Dirk?"

Chapter Eleven

Dirk slapped his hands on the table in front of me. "What the hell were you thinking?"

Ahh—old home week. We were back in the interrogation room he used the last time I got hauled in. I considered having an etched nameplate installed on the hard oak chair my butt filled.

"I don't believe I heard the question. Could you repeat it?"

"Don't play with me, Katie. It's two in the morning and I'm not in the mood for tall tales. Tell me what's going on right now or I'll toss you in a cell and forget about you. We pulled in a few female drunks from Johnny's. They'll be happy to keep you company for the next twelve hours."

I gulped. Johnny's had a reputation as the skankiest place in town. Day or night, its patrons were not my preferred choice as roommates. Even so, Dirk's implied threat ticked me off. "Give it up. You can't hold me without charging me, and I didn't do anything wrong."

"How about cemetery desecration and trespassing? Enough charges for you? We'll get a statement from the trucker who radioed in Ginger's car after he noticed flashlights in the locked cemetery." He stressed the word locked, and I barely kept from flinching.

"Then there are the recent chips in several gravestones that look suspiciously like bullet marks.

Our guys found shell casings under some big bushes."
He took a deep breath in a way that convinced me he
clung to the end of his hypothetical rope. "And we have
a bag full of money."

He glared at me. If I hadn't already used the
cemetery's bathroom, his narrowed eyes and pursed lips
would've scared the pee out of me. Another true Mrs.
Crankshaw moment.

My answer came out fast and shaky. "The
blackmailer threatened Ginger with Rob's life if we told
the cops about the pay off."

"You think we couldn't find a police woman to
make the drop for Ginger? Or couldn't place the Howes
in protective custody? Or quietly surround the cemetery
and catch the bastard?" He shoved the bag down the
table. "Now the sleaze is gone and we're no closer to
the killer." Dirk paced.

"You mean Morgan's killer and the blackmailer are
the same person?"

He swiveled. "That's not your business, is it?" He
sat and took my hands. "Katie, this isn't a television
show or a game. You were shot at and would have been
killed if the trucker hadn't noticed Ginger's car and your
flashlights."

His quiet tone after the outburst made my stomach
clench. "We were about to drop the money and leave
when the bullets flew. We didn't expect to get shot."
My voice sounded as small as I felt.

His last sentence finally penetrated and caught my
attention. "Hey, did the trucker see another car? The
blackmailer had to park somewhere."

He hesitated. "No, but we'll go back in a few hours
and check for tracks."

"Why were you there tonight? Isn't trespassing a routine patrol?"

"Just because I believe you're both innocent doesn't mean my boss does. I'm alerted if you get a parking ticket." Dirk pointed his index finger in my face. "Quit stalling. You need to tell me what's going on. Everything."

Eating cemetery dirt while shots winged overhead rendered me talkative. My story wouldn't have taken long to tell if Dirk hadn't interrupted me after every other sentence. When I finished my tale and answered his questions, I sat back exhausted. Dirk didn't look perky, either.

"I'm letting you go. I doubt we'll get any further tonight."

I sat up, happy to avoid Johnny's skanks.

"We'll place a guard on your house until further notice." My outraged gasp didn't sway him. "Look, shots were fired tonight. That's attempted murder. Neither you or Ginger will go unguarded on my watch, so get over your snit."

He left the room without another word.

I wanted to know what had happened that made him so protective of women, but didn't think he'd tell me any time soon.

****

Ginger sat at my kitchen table playing with a mug of cooling tea. We decided to tell Rob that Ginger had been with me. If he asked.

She said he wouldn't miss her, which made me wonder again why she stayed in a bad marriage. I clamped my mouth shut on that topic.

We were drinking chamomile to decompress. After

we got some sleep, Ginger would go home and I'd log a few hours at work. If I didn't go in, Jim would blow up my computer trying to maintain the workload.

"What do you think will happen with the blackmailer? Do you think I'll get another note?"

I could tell she worried Rob could be in danger, and I didn't have answers. "Let Dirk worry about that. If another note comes, you promised to turn it over to him, remember?"

We sat in near silence. Her wrinkled forehead and periodic sniffling told me all I needed to know about her state of mind.

She sipped. "We know we aren't Morgan's murderers. I wonder if the killer didn't mean to take Morgan's life. Maybe he or she just wanted to make him sick."

I hated to burst Ginger's rose-colored bubble, but I did. "Dirk said the evidence points to premeditated."

"Oh."

Yep, there wasn't much to say faced with that fact. "I vote for Flash as the perp."

Ginger's lips picked up at the corners. "You really don't like her, do you?"

"Nope." Exhaustion precluded saying more.

She pushed her mug away. "I didn't realize Justin and Morgan were business partners.

"Justin always kissed up to Morgan. From all I've heard, Morgan was the draw. Without him, the studio will probably go under."

That tidbit made my ears perk up. "Really? That's too bad."

Ginger frowned. "Why's that?"

"Because Justin is my next favorite choice for

killer." *Right after Rob.* "Running errands when Morgan died doesn't rule him out. I wonder, though, if he's enough of a maniac to leave a poisoned mat laying around for someone else to grab by mistake." I also wondered why I gave Justin any kind of break. He was right behind Flash on my "people I liked the least" list. No, actually they were in a tie for top position. Good memories kept Rob from that spot.

Ginger didn't answer right away. "What if Justin did lace the mat with poison earlier that morning? Then he left on a fake errand so he'd have an alibi."

"Are you saying no one else ever touched Morgan's mat or blocks?"

She nodded a yes. "He stored his equipment separately."

"So a class member wouldn't get Morgan's mat by mistake?"

"That's right. You were the only new person at class that morning. Everyone else had their own mat and blocks."

"So Justin could have poisoned Morgan's equipment."

"Justin or anyone who arrived early. They left the door unlocked for people who wanted to meditate before class."

I snapped my fingers and Ginger's head jerked. "The killer could be Flash after all."

Ginger's cheeks got a tinge of color. "Yep."

My laptop beckoned. I sipped lukewarm tea as the machine booted up.

"What are you doing?"

"A good authority told me you can find anything on the Internet. I figure we should find out how the poison is applied and how long until the dose takes effect."

Ginger looked suitably impressed, and within five minutes of start-up, I'd found the information. "Says here, ricin made from castor beans can kill in as little as thirty minutes. No longer than an hour. Causes people to upchuck."

She ignored my slang and focused on the meaty information. "Do side-effects depend on body size, fitness or immunity?"

Not just a pretty face, my BFF. She looked over my shoulder and we scanned articles together.

She whistled. "Doesn't take much to kill someone. A half an aspirin's worth?" She sat like her knees gave out. "And ricin can be ingested, inhaled or injected? The poison must have been in his mat."

I couldn't affirm her idea without giving away that Dirk entrusted me with the same information. Her pale face and shaky voice bothered me.

"Still bugs me that he looked so peaceful when I walked by him. And even though he vomited, the volume was limited."

Ginger grinned. "You never were any good with science." She rested her chin on her palm. "Not only is each body different, if Morgan absorbed a large amount of ricin, his respiratory distress could have happened faster than the nausea." She paused and looked thoughtful. "Also, Morgan drank peppermint and ginger based teas exclusively. That herb and spice are used to treat nausea. They may have suppressed the drug-induced side effects."

"Was there an earlier class that day?"

"No. Saturday classes always started with the one

we attended."

"And you were a regular?"

Her soft voice shakes again. "Yes. For months."

I didn't want to voice my thoughts, but I saw Ginger hopscotch to my conclusion ahead of me. "Someone wanted you to witness his death, maybe get blamed for the murder."

Ginger's eyes watered. She wiped them with the back of her sleeve. "But why?"

"I think someone knew Morgan really wanted to run off with you and didn't like it. Not at all."

"No way." She denied the idea before I finished speaking.

"Listen. This makes sense." Too bad Morgan screwed most of the class. Sifting through the potential jealous lovers could take weeks. And worse, the scenario didn't eliminate Rob.

"Katie, I think that's far-fetched."

I looked away because I could see the potential of Rob's involvement hadn't escaped her. She needed a diversion.

"I knew it was Flash!"

This time Ginger didn't smile. Her thoughtful expression told me she understood someone hated her enough to want her dead.

I pulled out my stash of chocolate-covered mint cookies and placed one of the cellophane packs in front of her. She didn't say a word but opened the bag and ate each and every cookie.

****

"So Flash and Justin could have worked together to kill Morgan." I finished my spiel and checked Dirk's face for a reaction.

I'd stopped by after pushing out the most important work for Jim. On my way home, I decided to lay my ideas out for Dirk. A frown and rapidly tapping fingers didn't signal the reaction I'd envisioned.

He leaned across the narrow conference room table as Matt entered. "What part of 'stay out of this case' can you not comprehend?"

Matt dropped a short stack of case files on the table and squeezed my shoulder. "I think you've come up with a great theory." Too bad he didn't stay to defend me, instead of running from the room.

Dirk threw a dirty look at his partner's back then turned the glower on me. "I've told you before. You're not a trained detective."

"So you won't check out my ideas? I still say both Justin and Flash had opportunity."

"We're already checking them out." He ran a hand through his choppy hair. "No motives. With Morgan gone, Justin is left with a failed investment. Doesn't make good business sense to kill his partner."

"Flash has a motive. I've heard she was really pissed Morgan dumped her for Ginger."

He sat back in his chair and leaned his head on his hand. "Brandi Wells doesn't strike me as a woman who'd dirty her hands."

"If she hired someone, you could still get her for conspiracy to murder, right?"

His lips quirked. "You really don't like Ms. Wells, do you?"

Why did people keep asking me that question? "Do you?"

He tried unsuccessfully to hold back his smile. "I keep my distance from murder suspects. Just a little trick I learned over the years."

"So that means I'm not a suspect?" I clapped my hand over my mouth. My high school teachers told me to engage my brain first then speak. Something I've never learned.

Dirk's eyes looked sad. "Sorry, my boss still has a soft spot for your guilt. You didn't happen to go to school with him, or maybe date him, did you? It's almost like he has a vendetta for you."

"Funny man."

Dirk did his waiting for an answer thing, so I obliged. "What's his name?" I waited until he opened his mouth and then spoke over him. "No, I don't know your boss. Give me a break. Am I that big of a disaster?"

I hoped his response, unfavorable to the disaster appellation, would go unvoiced. Allen walked in followed by Matt. "We've got a lead on those tracks." Allen noticed me and halted. "Sorry, I didn't see Katie with you."

Dirk escorted me to the door. "I think we're finished, Ms. Sheridan. Thanks for your insights." His next sentence was under his breath. "Stay out of this and don't forget to lock your damn door."

He turned and addressed the two officers. "So what did you get?"

Dirk didn't close the door fast enough. Just before it clicked shut I heard, "Mid-sized bike."

Crap. Just when I thought Rob couldn't be involved. Parked in Ginger's garage stood a mid-sized Ducati motorcycle. Even though Rob had morphed into super asshole, I hoped he didn't kill Morgan. If only for Ginger's sake.

Chapter Twelve

Dirk waited at my door. Tantalizing aromas of hot cheese and sausage wafted from the cardboard box he held.

"What are you doing here?"

He pushed the pizza box toward me like a sacrificial offering. "I came to apologize."

I crossed my arms over my chest. "Too little, too late, Buster. Besides, it's kind of late."

"Just got off work."

His exhausted demeanor primed me to nurture him. I got over the urge. My Mama taught me to restrict my mothering to the boys I birthed.

"I brought ice cream." He held up a plastic grocery bag jammed with pint-sized containers. I could see the distinctive Ben & Jerry's covers. If he brought Chunky Monkey, he was in.

"There's Chunky Monkey, Cinnamon Buns and Cherry Garcia. And another one I can't remember."

I grabbed the bag. "I guess you can come in." Moving down the hall, I finalized my decision. "You can have the Cherry Garcia."

The dead bolt clicked home and I felt a bout of warm and fuzzy come over me. I pulled out my two best plates—no chips—and I took the one with a slight crack. A longneck came out of the fridge for Dirk, but I stuck to water. No telling when he'd go into cop mode, and I still hadn't caught up on my sleep.

"So do you want to chit chat or eat?"

Dirk's eyes glazed over. "Eat." He packed away three slices of pizza before coming up for air and a pull at the beer.

"Feeling better?"

He leaned forward. "I'd feel a hell of a lot better if I knew you'd leave this case alone. It's screwy. The pieces aren't coming together, and I've got a gut feel the murderer is biding his time."

The pizza I'd eaten threatened to make a repeat appearance. "What do you mean?"

He put his hand over mine. "I mean the murderer isn't done. He's after you or Ginger or both of you. I can't figure why, but that's how it feels to me."

His thumb drew lazy circles over my wrist. He lifted his gaze to mine. "I'd hate that, Katie. More than I can say."

"Does your boss still have me pegged as the killer?"

"Not now."

"What changed his mind?"

Dirk shrugged.

A breath I didn't know I held slipped out between my lips. "Good." I had to ask, though I didn't expect an answer. "Do you think the blackmailer will send another note?" A more important question surfaced. "Could the blackmailer and murderer be the same person?"

He hesitated. "You're not a suspect, but I can't discuss anything else with you. I stopped by to apologize, but also because I want you and Ginger to be on your guard. Always. Don't cross the street without looking both ways four times. Keep your doors locked. Be aware of the vehicles around you on the street. All that and more. This isn't over."

I shuddered. Dirk grasped my hand. He leaned forward while pulling me toward him and we met in a savory tasting of pizza-flavored lips. Sounds kinda yucky, but boy, oh boy.

"We're keeping someone outside your house, but the department can't afford that much longer."

What Dirk didn't say was that his boss decided I'm not a suspect, so the guard they had on me to prevent flight wasn't needed.

He wrapped his fingers in my hair. "Enough about the case."

His actions in bringing pizza weren't totally altruistic. I decided to confront him before he distracted me. "Dirk, why are you here?"

"I told you. I'm apologizing for being rude today."

"Don't think so." We leaned back and stared at each other across the table.

He blew out a breath. "Okay, out with it."

Taking a big breath, I jumped in with both feet. "You've made references to women not getting hurt while you're on the job. What happened? Why does this subject eat at you?"

He chugged some beer and I figured he bought time while deciding what to tell me. It's what I'd do in his place.

Dirk cleared his throat. "I worked in Charlotte before moving here. My familiarity with big city crime made me attractive to the chief." He tapped his fingers against his lips. "That same experience was my reason for moving here."

Raw pain flashed across his face in a quick spasm. Warm gestures are not my thing, but I moved to put my hand over his. He grasped it like a safety line.

"You look a little like her, my last partner in Charlotte." Our gazes met. "Amy Porter. Not long out of the Academy, and paired with me when my former partner retired."

"We had what we thought was a routine call. Domestic disturbance, but everyone knows those can get ugly." He interlaced his fingers with mine.

"Took a little while, but we got the husband and wife separated, relieved their weapons and talked until they cooled down." He contemplated our intertwined fingers then sipped at his beer. I committed to giving him all the time he needed, but he continued almost at once.

"Amy was perfect. Her defusing technique was awesome to watch, especially impressive in a rookie."

His hand trembled. I squeezed his fingers and he gave me a faint smile. Dirk sipped beer then pushed the half-empty bottle to the side.

"It all fell apart. The husband came charging back into the kitchen, grabbed Amy by the hair and pulled a knife from the counter, all before I could make a move."

My throat closed and my eyes were sandy. I felt out of control, like watching a car accident.

Dirk swallowed. "I thought I'd confined him, but the damn lock didn't work."

His grip tightened. My physical discomfort couldn't match his emotional hurt.

He rubbed his crooked nose with his free hand. "Amy didn't make it. Our backup unit pulled me off the guy before I killed him, but it was a near thing. I took a leave, and then I left."

We sat quietly, or at least I did. No telling what roiled through Dirk. I hoped I helped by being with him. I couldn't ever understand his experience, but when he told me to lock my damn door, I would. A little part of me questioned whether he was attracted to me because I reminded him of Amy. I didn't want to examine that idea.

He took a quick sip of his beer and set it aside. "I didn't mean to tell you all that."

I nodded, not trusting my voice, but that seemed to suffice.

"Your turn. You're gorgeous. You had a polite divorce. Why do you store your fancy wine glasses?"

My eye roll and snort didn't seem to count as an answer he'd accept. Too bad, because I wasn't ready to say more. Trust people? Not hardly.

"Okay, fine if you don't want to tell me."

His hurt tone put me over the edge. "I'm an orphan." I kept my head down. Crap. I was telling a story I didn't discuss with many people. My curiosity got the best of me and I peeked at his expression.

His steady gaze held not a hint of pity and that helped me continue. "I bounced between relatives until Aunt Myrtle accepted guardianship." I gulped. "Took me awhile to figure out she wanted the insurance money my folks left."

Dirk's quiet presence and his total concentration on me made me realize I could get through the telling. "She moved into our house here in town and took over everything." I pushed my familiar anger down. "Myrtle could have been the prototype for Jabba the Hut. She sat her fat butt in my mother's favorite chair like a malignant spider. If I got too close, she'd smack me upside the head or pinch me."

I felt like a babbler, like a jackhammer punched my heart and all the anger and pain surged out. I caught his gaze and level regard. Good thing he didn't show sympathy. I'd have crawled in a hole for the next twenty years.

My throat closed and I cleared it. "She was clever, my aunt. Told me if I reported her hitting me no one would believe a kid over an adult. She knew how to hit and pinch so the marks didn't show. I learned to keep my distance, but that only infuriated her." I tried for humor. "Did you know I have eyes in the back of my head?"

His lips quirked, but he didn't smile.

"I ran away, but the cops brought me back." More than once, which is why I never warmed to the men in blue. Not to mention they'd been the ones to take me to Protective Services the night my parents died.

"How old were you when you ran the first time?"

Smart man. Not only did he figure I ran, he knew it had to be more than once. "Fifteen." I paused to swallow a lump. "Ginger was my friend before my parents died, and she knew what was going on. She's always known everything about me. She got her mom on my side, but you know how it was. Years ago, kids didn't have the protection they do now. And Myrtle knew how to suck up to people in power."

Dirk's growl surprised me. "Is your aunt still alive?"

"No, she spent all the insurance money, died and went to hell, I hope." My energy faded and I sagged against the back of my chair. I felt lighter, even though I didn't admit to all the hurt Myrtle had inflicted. That'd be too much.

He ran the back of his hand across my cheek. "We're carrying around a lot of baggage, aren't we?"

Boy Howdie. He didn't whistle Dixie.

He reached for his ringing cell phone. A quick number check and he walked away, flipping open his phone. I couldn't hear words, but knew from the tone the call had to be business.

"Look, I'm sorry, but I gotta go." He pulled me close, grasped the back of my neck and kissed me like he really was sorry about leaving. As if the message wasn't clear, he nibbled at my bottom lip before pulling away at snail speed.

"Save me some dessert, will ya? If it's not too late, I'd like to come back after I finish up at the office." His tongue in my mouth told me didn't lie.

He lifted his mouth to change the angle of his kiss and I took the opportunity to answer his question. "Like I said, the Cherry Garcia is all yours. If you're good, you can have the Cinnamon Buns too."

"Is that all you're willing to give?"

Dirk's talented digits moved south. Under his fingers, my ass didn't feel too big at all. I wasn't ready to answer his question, so I let my hands do a little roaming of their own.

We were both breathing hard and broke apart to inhale.

"So you're strictly a chocolate loving woman?"

"In some things, yes."

With that out of the way, we got back to swapping saliva.

He brushed my hair back, leaving his palms cradling my face. "I shouldn't be here, but I can't leave."

"It's not a good idea to kiss a witness in an open case, is it? Or am I a person of interest?"

"Some things are worth breaking the rules."

I ignored my hormones, and his non-answer. I did the smart thing and stepped out of his embrace. Damn it. "Go answer your call. We've got time."

Dirk's disappointed look inflamed my ego. "Yeah, you're right." He walked to the door, me following every delicious move of his tush. He struck a pose and with a bad Schwarzenegger imitation said, "I'll be back." He winked and sauntered out the door then stuck his head back inside. "And lock the damn door so I can hear it happen."

Be still my rampaging heart.

****

"You sound out of breath. Did you run for the phone expecting a call from Dirk, or did you drag out your kickboxing DVD again?"

Ginger's tone sounded almost normal; a welcome change from her silent cookie-eating meltdown. I turned off the muted TV and slid the exercise video out of the DVD player. "Damn, you interrupted us."

"Really? Sorry, I'll call back."

"Don't hang up. I'm kidding and ready for a break." That was no lie. It had been impossible to relax after Dirk left; too many crazed hormones flying around. It was either find a skank bar and hope for a random pick-up or exercise until my lust simmered down and—I hoped—Dirk returned. If I'd gone to Johnny's Bar, the sweat trickling down my back would be from a much different cause, and fighting my way to the bar for a drink would be the only reason to be breathless. Not that I'd willingly go to Johnny's in this lifetime.

"So was I right?"

"You're usually right. What about this time?"

"A little bird told me Dirk visited your house earlier."

A snort escaped my mouth before I could suppress it. "Little bird, hell. Why didn't you just park and come in?"

My friend's voice lost its cheery flavor. "I didn't want to interrupt."

"Ginger, what's wrong? Did you and Rob fight?"

"No fight. He's gone."

My ears seemed plugged. Had she said Rob was gone? "You mean he's not home from work yet?"

Her tone sounded dead. "No, I mean gone."

"I'll be right over." No way I wanted Ginger sitting alone in that big old house.

Should I leave a note for Dirk in case he returned? Did that count as presumptuous, wishful thinking, or smart? Phoning him at work wouldn't happen. He got called in and didn't need me giving him detailed movement information. I mean, where would it stop? When I went to the bathroom? Gross.

I settled for a note inside a sealed envelope addressed to him and tacked to the front door. The short distance to my friend's house seemed like a trip across country. She opened the door right after my car pulled into her driveway and walked out to greet me.

We hugged. "Hey, sweetie. I brought Chunky Monkey and Thin Mints."

"Dirk has you figured out, hasn't he?"

My back went up. "Whadda mean by that?"

She put her arm through mine and pulled me toward her front door. "You don't buy Chunky Monkey for yourself unless you're PMSing, and I know your cycle because it's the same as mine. That means someone gave you the ice cream unless you stopped on the way, and you got here too fast for a grocery trip. Sooo, I'm voting Dirk."

"B&J could have been on sale and I stocked up."

"No sale and it wasn't in your freezer when you gave me cookies the other day."

My arm dropped from hers. "Damn, you are one scary woman."

She closed the door behind us and leaned against it. "So am I right?"

"Yes, doggone you."

She gave me a small smile. "Well, at least something's going right for one of us."

I searched her expression, but didn't find any answers there. "Tell me."

We walked to the kitchen. Ginger had tea steeping. She grabbed two mugs and we settled at the table. There'd be no standing on ceremony tonight, not that we ever did.

She hogged the Chunky Monkey in a way that told me she wasn't ready to talk. Halfway through the pint, she put down her spoon. "I think Rob's gone for good."

Her hand laid palm up on the table so I covered it with mine. "What makes you say that? Did you see him go?"

She muttered a "no."

"Did he leave a note? Call?"

"No. He said nothing." She answered my unvoiced

question. "His toiletries are gone and so are some of his favorite clothes."

My chest relaxed. "He probably had to take a quick business trip. I bet he'll call you later tonight." The idea sounded weak. I wished I knew how to make Ginger's pain disappear.

Her eyes focused on a point over my shoulder. "You know, I'm not so sure I care if he calls or not."

"Why not?"

She turned her full attention on me. "I love Rob. It's just that I don't know if I can stay married to him."

The words echoed through my brain. I'd said almost the same thing to Ginger when my own marriage fell apart. Remembered hurt combined with fresh pain to fill the room. I ripped open the cookie package. Forget aspirin. Emotional relief is best handled with large doses of chocolate.

"If he did leave—"

"He's gone."

Her monotone indicated she'd stopped trying to improve a sucky situation. "Where do you think he went? He wouldn't bunk with the And Howes, would he?"

Rob's mother always abbreviated her husband Andrew's name to And. when she wrote return addresses. When I originally saw her notation on Ginger and Rob's rehearsal dinner invitation, I showed Ginger and her in-laws had been the And Howes ever since.

"Mrs. H would add a suite to the house if it meant she had her 'Precious' back in her nest."

I steered Ginger away from the landmine that was the And Howes. "So he took some clothes, toiletries, and his car. Anything else missing that could be a clue?"

The color her cheeks had gained with judicious application of excess sugar, paled. She jumped from her chair and ran to Rob's study, me in her wake. Her shaking hands caused a loud clatter as she rifled through a desk drawer.

"Where's the damn key?

"Let me help. What kind of key is it?"

"The one for the gun safe."

My hands turned into ice cubes. "I didn't know you had a gun in the house."

"I didn't. Rob did."

So few words, such a big gulf to jump.

"Got it." She held up a small silver color key. Moving to the bookcase, she tossed a framed wedding photo on the floor without looking at it. Ginger and Rob's happy expressions, frozen in time, looked out from behind cracked glass. I turned my attention back to Ginger. My already upset stomach clenched.

She had the door to the small gun safe open. It was empty.

Chapter Thirteen

I didn't think the night could get worse. Silly me. I needed to stop taunting the universe. Ginger refused to talk about Rob or the missing gun. She ignored my pleading and refused to report his disappearance to the police. When I pushed, she kicked me out. We'd never had such an unreasonable fight. The unreality of the evening's events left me stunned.

Returning home alone thirty minutes later, I saw a suspicious shape in my drive. A dark-colored car parked so close to my neighbor's hedge, I almost didn't notice the vehicle. I slowed but didn't pull in the drive. A mini-panic attack rolled over me until Dirk stepped away from the shrubbery.

He opened the passenger side door and slid in. "I told you to lock your doors and take precautions. Do I have to spell out every move for you? And why the hell did you leave a note giving your location? Do you want the killer to come after you? Or me?"

My unsettled nerves chose anger as a vehicle for a release. "Get over yourself, Johnson." I showed him the can of pepper spray I held. "I'm prepared. I don't need a babysitter."

He disarmed me with a quick move and held the nozzle toward me, his finger on the triggering mechanism. "This thing could be used against you that easily. Stop taking risks, Katie."

Dirk tossed the canister into my lap. "I'll wait while you park the car." He exited, slamming the car door behind him.

My throat didn't want to swallow the crow I'd just eaten, but I forced down the feathers and pulled next to his vehicle. I locked the car and stalked to my front door. Silly me. Instead of feeling relieved Dirk watched over me, I was peeved. It felt kind of like having my parents back, but different. My thoughts were all messed up, and it was easier to blame Dirk for the confusion than to figure it out.

He moved to my side, waited until I unlocked the door then pushed past me to enter first. I entertained snarky comments about Mr. Manners when he pulled his gun.

"Something doesn't smell right. Wait by the door and be ready to run."

No way. If someone got past Dirk, they'd be on me like sticky tarpaper coated a new roof. I crept behind him as he moved through the rooms, checking human-sized hiding places.

I noticed obvious signs of an intruder before we even reached the kitchen. The sight of my favorite room almost made my heart stop. All the dishes in my glass-door cabinets littered the heart pine floor in shards. Every piece of glassware was smashed except a few items of Fiesta Ware and a Manhattan Glass serving plate. My back door stood wide open, and a variety of bugs flew around the room. Moths batted against the ceiling light. Some field mice probably snuck in to join the party too.

A message waited for me, written in what looked like bright red lipstick and centered on my fridge's freezer door.

You're next.

Damn it. I'd just bought that fridge. It'd take me elbow grease I didn't want to burn to wipe that crap off. Plus I had a stomach full of knots. What exactly did the nut job mean? Because the mess I looked at almost made me cry. And that said a lot.

Picking up an iron fry pan, I held my pepper spray ready and crunched to the door. Dirk got there before me, shutting it quietly. He put a finger to his lips. I hadn't heard him coming. Talk about too little, too late.

Dirk pulled me behind him with a stern look and we continued the room-by-room search. By accident or unconscious design, we were standing in my bedroom when he holstered his gun.

My arms crossed over my chest in a comforting self-hug. "Weren't you supposed to call for back up?"

Dirk looked around the room. "Yeah, but I was hoping to catch the shithead so I could push his face in the floor first." He put his attention on me and waited.

"Look, I don't want you taking risks for me."

Dirk gave me a look I couldn't read before he shrugged.

Not satisfied, I pushed. "Why'd you come back tonight?"

He sauntered closer and ran his hand over my hair. "We have unfinished business."

"More interrogation?"

"Oh, yeah."

His lips moved over mine and his form of questioning could send the female half of the world into a crime spree. Including happily married women, honest.

The bubble burst when he spoke. "Throw some stuff in a bag. You've got to get out of here tonight."

My head still reeled from the kiss, so I didn't understand what I'd heard. "Excuse me?"

"Look, this guy is telling you he can get at you any time. You can't stay here."

I pulled out of his embrace with a jerk. "What are you, the Lone Ranger? This is my home. Sure, it's a mess, but it's mine." I planted my fists on my hips. "What can this guy do that he hasn't already tried or done?"

"Succeed."

That one word stymied all my thoughts. I pushed my way through the paralysis and came up with some words. "If that lipstick is a clue, the intruder was a crazy woman. I vote for Flash."

"The writing looked like a guy's scrawl to me. Stay with me."

"Don't you think your invitation's a little sudden? We haven't even made love yet." Oops. What if his offer meant his couch or guest room?

"It will happen. Admit it. You couldn't keep your eyes off me at the studio. Just a matter of time till we do the deed."

"You must not have heard me. Men in blue aren't my favorite people." Arrogant ass. Okay, so I've checked his butt out once or twice. How did he see me do it? Too bad he can read me like a grad student with a grade school primer.

"I'm not wearing blue." He ran the back of his fingers across my cheek. "You're not safe here."

I shivered. That was the truth and the reality pissed me off. I loved my sweet little mess of a bungalow.

"Don't even try to argue. Get your stuff while I call this in."

Did I say arrogant ass? Let me add high-handed, big-headed, over-bearing and - and - I need a thesaurus. Oh, yeah. Over-confident and pushy.

"Okay, look. Maybe staying with me isn't the best option right now."

"Ya think?"

"Would Ginger have room in the McMansion for you? Or do you not get along with her husband?"

Tell him or not? My mouth made the decision for me. "Rob's gone."

"What? You should have told me." The growl coming out of his mouth gave me shivers, and not in a good way.

"Just happened. He left tonight."

Dirk snapped open his phone and turned his back on me. I didn't know which hurt more, his anger or his cold shoulder. Maybe both caused the burning in my chest.

"Matt, we've got a runner. Rob Howe. He's around six two, one-ninety, blue eyes. Hell, just get his DMV photo into circulation." He turned to me. "What does he drive?" To my blank look he said, "Telling me is faster than looking up their vehicles. At least it would be if you'd answer."

"He took his new car this morning, a white Mercedes SL class." Good thing I'd asked Ginger. They'd be looking for the right auto instead of putting out an alert on all the models stored in her five-car garage.

"Don't forget the Homeland Security travel restriction and get someone tracking his credit cards.

140

Wait a minute." Dirk stopped for a breath.

"Matt, see if you can get a read on his vehicle." His phone clicked shut and he turned toward me. "The government never should have discontinued the Space Program."

The sudden detour threw me. "What does NASA have to do with tracking a fugitive?"

"Where do you think all our technology came from? But first we need to get you someplace safe." He moved in. "I promise I'll make you feel better."

Maybe the kitchen mess had scrambled my brain, but before we went further, I needed to clear the air. "Dirk, are you interested in me because I look like Amy?"

"You're not her."

I stepped back. "You're not her," was not what I'd wanted to hear. My body language must've telegraphed that because he pulled me back into the circle of his arms.

"There's a slight resemblance. Your similarities surprised me at first, but that's not why I'm here."

"So, why?"

He nuzzled my neck. "Sex. Well, sex and I want to protect you. At least I do when you're not off wielding a fry pan."

"It's not fair for you to bring it up. I wouldn't have to carry a fry pan if people would stop breaking into my house."

His lips moved to my ear lobe. "And that brings me to my next point."

"Only one?"

He moved his lips to my neck. If we weren't having a serious conversation, his action would have my knees collapsing. "Call Ginger. Ask her to let you stay with her."

"Don't worry about me. I'll find a place to stay."

He pulled away from my neck, leaving disappointment behind. His eyes narrowed. "What are you not telling me?"

My throat needed clearing. "We had a fight. Ginger kicked me out."

"That does it. You're coming with me. Find a bag." He yanked open a drawer. Of course, he chose the one holding my "someday my Prince will come underwear." His hand stilled on the black satin Teddy, then he scooped the lingerie and added a few more choice numbers to his grasp. His eyes were dark when his gaze met mine. "Got that bag ready, yet?"

I looked at his satin and silk filled hands. No contest. I grabbed a duffel bag off the closet shelf. It wasn't imported leather but it got the job done.

The doorbell rang. He stuffed my underwear in the bag and stalked from the room, his packing done. Men.

My packing didn't take long, either. I swung the bag onto my shoulder and headed into the kitchen. I said hello to the crime scene techs moon-suiting their way into my kitchen. My neighbors could have a field day analyzing all the activity in my little bungalow. I'd rather they had something else to gossip about.

Dirk stood to one side speaking in a low voice with Matt. Their conversation broke off when I joined them but I heard one phrase that chilled me. "His alibi doesn't check."

Were they talking about Rob or someone else?

"So, Matt, I need you to handle this. I'm taking Ms. Sheridan to a friend's house."

Matt looked me over and smirked. "Maybe you should stop by Urgent Care and get that neck bruise checked out, first." He pointed to my left side.

I slapped a hand over my neck. My face heated and I turned an angry stare on Dirk. What the hell did he do? Mark me? That was so high school.

Matt laughed, punched Dirk on the arm and turned away. We left and none too soon. I decided I should have packed some everyday underwear because my Prince remained a frog.

We climbed into his car and he pulled out of the drive, all in silence.

"Why didn't you tell me you'd left marks? I'd have changed my top." Our mutual passion, on top of the intruder, left me discombobulated. Otherwise I'd have ripped him a new one.

"Heat of the moment. That bruise came up fast. I didn't notice."

My eyes narrowed and I knew smoke poured out of my ears like a cartoon character. Did I see a smirk on his too handsome face? Retribution was mine, and it was gonna be hell. On him.

We pulled onto a street in a quiet neighborhood I remembered from my childhood. The houses hadn't changed much, gentrified but still solid working class houses with good-sized yards. Developers went with the rich farmland on the outskirts of town, and that's where Ginger's McMansion was located. Dirk's neighborhood spoke to my middle class soul and soothed me.

He parked in front of a small Cape Cod. The yard had nice plantings, but the grass needed a cutting. The house looked less than two thousand square feet with a master on the first floor and two slanted ceiling bedrooms boasting small dormer windows upstairs. The main floor likely held a small living room, eat-in kitchen and bath besides the master. That was my assessment until we entered.

The tiny rooms and dark interior I envisioned didn't exist. Instead, thanks to a tasteful addition at the back, he had an open floor plan with lots of windows. Sparse furniture with a masculine feel and size fit the house. The couch looked like I could stretch out and get in a solid eight hours. I plopped my butt onto it, duffel at my feet. "Nice couch. You have a blanket and pillow I can use?"

"Nope."

"No?" I hid a smile. My heart and lots of other places did a happy dance.

"I've got a guest room upstairs. Has a bed and attached bath. You can stay there."

The happy dance died a strangled death. "Okay, that works for me."

"Unless—"

I held my breath. We hadn't known each other long, but Dirk read me better than anyone except Ginger.

His hand snaked out and wrapped around the back of my neck. His lips were on mine and I forgot about the awkwardness of being in his home for the first time, the mess at my bungalow and the killer. Everything melted away in the heat of a tongue-tangling kiss. Happy moans filled the room, all from my throat.

Dirk ran his fingertips over my forehead, smoothed my eyebrows then rubbed my cheekbones. His thumb caressed my lips and I arched my back, pushing my already tightened nipples against his chest. He dipped his head, replacing his thumb with his lips. There were more happy moans and shameless arching on my part.

My fingers moved into his hair and massaged his head. It was Dirk's turn to moan, thank you very much. Gratified with his response, my hand massaged the knots in his neck and shoulders. His muscles loosed under my fingers. Gee, guess I could have an alternative career if construction slowed down any more.

He moved his mouth to my ear and I couldn't help it. I moved my head to the side just in case he wanted to do some in-depth work in the area. He did, thank you God of Love. His licks and nibbles set up a heat wave. I wondered how long it'd be before I went up in flames.

He must have felt the heat. "I think you've been a bad girl."

"Me?" What, he wanted to question me about the murder again? Damn. Things were just getting good.

"Mm-hmm. I should do a strip search. You could be hiding weapons. Drugs."

"Isn't that the job of a female officer?"

His head jerked up and his gaze searched mine. "Are you not interested or are you saying you're into kinky stuff?"

I pulled his head back down and sucked his bottom lip. "Interested. Definitely interested."

Chapter Fourteen

Dirk rolled off me with a satisfied grunt. From him it sounded sexy.

My heart pounded and I was slick with sweat and other bodily fluids. When he shifted, a chill moved across my body.

He lay on his side, elbow crooked, head propped on his hand. "I knew you had weapons and drugs on you."

I arched my back, my hand trailed across my forehead. "So are you taking me in, detective?"

He ran his free hand across my boobs then trailed his fingers down my chest to my stomach. "Not yet. I'd better do a cavity search to make sure you aren't hiding more." His search took his hand to my curls, where his fingers kept his promise.

My hips came off the bed.

"If you get unruly, I may have to handcuff you."

"I promise I'll be good."

He leaned over me, his lips hovering over mine. "Just remember I'm watching your every move."

Untold minutes later I screamed, "I'll be good." Another big O ripped through me.

Role playing. Gotta love it.

****

I was up and moving slow, but the coffee helped. Dirk drove off at dawn, leaving me a big glass of ice water on the night table. I hoped Jim hadn't messed up too much at my desk. After two hours of sleep, my synapses weren't firing the way they should.

The Get Solid trailer was silent when I got there, but not for long. My outraged howl filled the room when I saw my desk. Or what would be a workspace if it weren't covered with a pile of project plans.

"I knew you couldn't stay away. Thanks for coming in, Katie." Jim stood behind me. My howl covered the sound of the door and his footsteps.

"What did you do to my desk?"

"Um, sorry?"

His sheepish grin might work with his wife, but cute doesn't cut it with me. "Jim, what were you thinking? Or were you thinking?" I ran my hands through my hair and hit a snarl. "Ouch. You didn't try to run the Auto-CAD, did you?"

He ducked his head and my questions. "Are you sure you should be in today? You look a little rough around the edges. Maybe you should take today off and I'll clean some of this up."

I debated the intelligence of yelling at my boss for making a mess of my desk after he gave me time off because I was involved in a murder. As I tried to consider all the ramifications of what should have been a simple question, three of the supervisors tromped in.

"Hey, Katie. What happened to your neck? Looks like you backed into the wrong set of teeth."

Cam grinned. "Her neck? What about her cheeks? That's beard burn if you ask me."

My fists went to my hips in defense mode. "I'm sorry I gave you pointers on proposing, Cam." I adjusted my collared tee and buttoned it. "By the way, how did it go? She say yes?"

Cam's grin got bigger. "Yep. Thanks, Katie. You're the bomb."

Tommy, the sheet rock supervisor, rubbed his hand over his mouth and tried to look serious but his eyes sparkled. "Speaking of bombs, did one go off in your bedroom?"

I braced myself. "Why do you think that, Tommy?"

Tommy pursed his lips in a silent whistle and looked to the ceiling. Maybe he prayed I didn't kill him after he spoke. "Your shoes don't match." He elbowed the other supervisor and they cracked up. "I thought maybe you couldn't find anything else to wear."

Crap. The supervisors were the last people I wanted noticing a tidbit like that, so I went on the offensive. "Actually, someone broke in last night and did a number on my kitchen."

Oh, boy. That did it. The testosterone level rose eighty degrees in thirty seconds. Jim responded first. "Katie, you come stay at my house. No one will get close with me and the dogs on guard."

Jim had a pack of the laziest bloodhounds in existence. Not only that, with his blood pressure, he couldn't be anywhere near stress, and that was my middle name.

I put my hand on his arm. "Thanks, Jim, but I'm fine."

"Sure, you're fine. You've got mismatched shoes, marks on your neck and burns on your face. What the hell?"

Should I tell him it was all self-invited? "Thanks, but I'm okay. Really. I may go stay with Ginger. She's got an alarm system."

The door opened. Matt and Dirk walked in as I finished my last sentence. Dirk knew I lied about staying with Ginger, but to his credit, didn't rat me out.

Jim frowned. "We're not hiring right now."

Matt stifled a grin behind his hand. "We already have jobs, Mr. Prestwick." He pulled his credentials holder from his pocket and showed his badge. "With Granville Falls Police Department."

Dirk's throat clearing made the only sound in the trailer. Even the sputtering coffee maker stopped brewing. "Ms. Sheridan, would you have a moment to speak with us about your report?"

Cam and Tommy nudged each other then Cam spoke. "You coming to ask her about the break-in last night? When you find the jerk that messed up her kitchen, let us know, will ya?"

Matt answered. "Justice will be served in court, guys."

Tommy's smirk made me wish I could run from the room. He was bound to embarrass me. "You should find the guy that gave her those beard burns on her face. Whoever it is needs some lessons in the right way to treat a lady."

What do you know? I was right. I prayed the floor would open to save me, but it remained solid. Crap.

Dirk's lips quirked at the corners. I didn't see another reaction. "Do you want to file another complaint, this one for assault? Or battery?"

I looked at Dirk then at his partner. Matt's eyes sparkled, daring me to answer. Dirk wore his stone face. I did what I do best. Ignored the question.

"Um, you said you had some questions to ask me?"

149

I turned to Jim, hoping my face wasn't as red as it felt. "Mind if we step outside for a minute?"

"Nope, go ahead." He grabbed Tommy and Cam by their necks and pointed them toward my desk. "You yahoos can help me straighten Katie's desk."

An eye roll and short walk later, I stood outside with Dirk and Matt. The sun burned hot.

"What's up?" I hoped my casual tone threw Matt off his hound dog scent.

"The crime scene report came in. No prints besides yours found in the kitchen. The intruder wore gloves."

I sighed. "Everyone wears gloves."

Dirk looked at his partner. "Can we have a minute?"

Matt shrugged and walked to their car, but not before I saw the smirk decorating his face.

"The offer to stay with me stands."

His words tempted me but if we lived together, even for a couple of days, we'd wear each other out. "Nope."

"That's it? You're not going to think about it?"

"Yep and nope."

His jaw tightened. "You're impossible." He turned on his heel then stopped and faced me again. "We could have something special, Katie, and you're too scared to give it a try."

"The other night you told me I'm not Amy. I see what you mean now. I'm just a cheap imitation."

"Katie, no."

"You turned your back on me to phone Matt when I was in the room. You don't want me to be part of this mess, but I'm in it up to my neck. Against my will, I might add. You want to make something with me?

Then treat me like I'm worthy of more than some hot sex and regular door locking orders."

His frown, tight shoulders, fisted hands and pursed mouth described his thoughts louder than words. He moved his head from side to side.

"I can't do that, Katie, and you shouldn't ask. A killer is after you and Ginger. Do you really think I'll expose you to that?" He took a step back. "Don't ask me to."

"Then we don't have much to say, do we?" I knew withdrawal was my normal response to overwhelming emotions. Feeling exposed made me squirm and look for escape routes.

A vulnerable look flashed across his face and disappeared so fast I thought it a trick of the light. Maybe we shared that trust problem.

"Guess not. Take care of yourself, okay?" He turned and walked away without looking back.

****

"I'm sorry." Ginger's subdued voice crossed the telephone line to my ear.

"So am I."

That's all we said. When words come from the heart, it doesn't take many to get the meaning across. I think I saw that on a greeting card.

Taking a deep breath, I asked, "How're you doing?"

"Let's see. I'm being blackmailed, my husband is gone and oh, yeah, I threw my best friend out of my life. Life could get worse, but I'd hate to be there."

Ginger. Master of the understatement.

"Mona called. Said we should stop by."

My mouth watered. Then it turned arid. If Mona

called wanting us to stop by, it meant she had some information. That could be good or bad.

We agreed to meet at the Chocolate Fix. Ginger waited outside the shop when I arrived. Walking in, we saw Mona waiting on a line of people and settled at a table to wait.

Ginger leaned toward me and lowered her voice. "Katie, I'm beginning to think Rob could be the person blackmailing me."

Finally. The suspicion I had running in my head was voiced. I treaded carefully because I didn't want to get pushed away again. "What makes you think that?"

"I haven't heard from him. Not a word."

"What else?"

"It's the business." She folded her hands in her lap.

Rob worked in finance, specializing in mergers and acquisitions. My gut roiled, a sure sign I didn't want to hear what she had to say.

"The quarterly investment report came today. Usually Rob takes care of that, but he's not here, so..."

So she wanted to know if Rob's flight involved money or another woman. Now my gut pumped like a butter churn on high.

"Rob put most of our money into a high-risk investment without telling me. We always shared decisions in the past."

Friendship shorthand filled in the rest. Rob took a flier with Ginger's money and screwed up. No wonder he ran.

"Did he, um...did he lose everything?"

"No. Mom taught me to diversify. Rob lost only a small portion of our net worth. I had left the rest with my Mom's advisers."

Shoot. Even if Rob wasn't the BM, my personal name for the nut job causing all these problems, he'd fallen into deep shit with Ginger. She remained the most forgiving person I knew. She'd had to be for us to stay friends all these years. But Rob would have to own up to his stupidity, and that wouldn't sit well with him. Maybe he was angry she wouldn't trust him with more of her money.

"Uh, Ginger, did he lose anywhere near a quarter mil?" A haunted gaze met mine across the table.

"That's it almost to a penny."

Crap. Things weren't looking good for Rob-boy.

A plate of truffles appeared magically before us. Mona slid into the remaining open chair. How much had she overheard? Her face appeared smooth and inscrutable. Hard to tell.

"Hey, girls. You up for some major gossip?"

"You bet." I forced my enthusiasm but Mona didn't appear to notice.

"Guess who's partnering with Justin?"

I blinked. "That's a loaded question. Do you mean partnering-lovers or business style?"

"Business." She shifted on her seat, something she only did when she had hot news.

"Oh, okay, that doesn't narrow down the gender." I made her squirm for about thirty seconds then relented. "I can't think of anyone," leaving out the words, "stupid enough."

"Brandi Wells is going in with Justin to run the Yoga Studio. They're reopening in a week, but are taking registrations now."

My mouth dropped open. I could feel it hanging there as if my jaw broke a hinge. "No."

"Yes."

Mona voiced my thoughts. "Why would she work? Her husband is loaded, right?"

"She probably wants to show off her boob job. Hanging out of her yoga togs is another opportunity." Okay, so I was jealous.

The storeowner looked thoughtful. "Could be she wants a piece of Morgan. Any way she can get one."

Ginger tapped her fingernail on the tabletop while eyeballing me. "She told me her husband travels a lot. Maybe she wants to stay busy."

I jumped in to erase her sudden lost look. "My, my, my. Flash and Justin. There's a match made in hell."

Mona laughed. "Got that right." She looked around the room and lowered her voice. "Word is the studio is broke. Justin lost his original investment and more."

Shocker alert. "Justin had the money? I thought Morgan headed the studio?"

Mona picked up a truffle and pushed the plate toward us. "Morgan was the public face, but he didn't invest a dime. Every penny came from Justin."

"So all the gifts, the request for studio rent, that all went in Morgan's pocket?"

"If the gossip is correct, that's right."

"The only way Justin could recoup his investment was to keep Morgan alive, then."

Mona leaned back in her chair. "Either that or cut his losses by ending the partnership."

Huh. That brought up another point. "Did they have a partnership agreement? You know, where Justin gets Morgan's stuff if he dies?"

She rested her chin on her palm. "I don't know, but I bet Brandi will get one from Justin. She's a bloodsucker."

We all nodded in unison.

"I did hear, though, that Morgan didn't have a will. They're trying to find his relatives, but none have come forward. So, I guess if there's no partner agreement, Justin is left in the cold."

"Well, he's got Flash." I paused for effect. "You're right. He's out in the cold." And scrambling to keep his head above water. I almost felt sorry for him, but the feeling didn't last long. He'd been a jerk.

"Katie, maybe we should sign up for yoga lessons."

Mona's eyes widened. "You two are riding for trouble."

Ginger answered before I could. "We're the Demonic Duo. We can do anything."

Chapter Fifteen

The Yoga Studio boasted a gaudy "Reopening Under New Management" sign. Okay, the sign was tasteful, but I didn't want to give credit to Flash. Or to Justin for that matter.

Ginger and I looked at the flapping canvas hung from the second story window. "Where are the skulls and crossbones? The beaker of poison? Shouldn't there be truth in advertising?"

She gave me an eye roll and we walked into the building. I hadn't been inside since Morgan's death. My heart beat faster, and not from climbing the stairs. Sure, I expected to feel some stress, but not the crushing darkness descending on me. I suspected the memory of feeling Morgan's heartbeats slow and stop would remain with me for a while.

Ginger walked in first, and I heard Brandi's gushy welcome. Flash's voice changed when she spotted me. Her lips twisted into a sneer that would make Mrs. Crankshaw proud. "Returning to the scene of the crime?"

My friend jumped in before I started a hair pulling catfight with the bitch in heat sitting at the desk. "We saw the sign. Congratulations on the reopening. Are you working here?"

Flash threw back her shoulders. "Partner."

Ginger didn't give away a thing. That's my BFF.

"Wow! Congratulations! I'm sure the Yoga Studio will prosper now that you're here."

I covered my mouth to hide a smile. Ginger could BS with the best of them.

"We'll be accepting only the best people as students." She appraised me with a look and I knew I wouldn't make the cut. Returning her gaze to Ginger, she smiled. "You're more than welcome, of course."

"Why thank you. Do you have a class price list?"

They got down to business and I wandered the area, trying to work out how the murderer could have accessed Morgan's mat and blocks. Pretty easy. A wide open area, the place where Morgan stored his equipment was clearly marked with a different color box and a sign noting it as personal. With the studio open early every Saturday, any number of people could have infused the mat with poison.

Anyone could have, but only a few people would. Maybe one of the women Morgan swindled, but I'd determined that wasn't a strong lead. The list of potential killers came down to just a few people and Rob topped it. Justin didn't seem likely, but I included him, and put Flash on the list out of spite. I wanted to see her in Jailhouse Orange.

"What is that woman doing here?" Uh, oh. Justin walked in, in full scream. Lucky no one else was in the studio with us.

He stormed to the desk and, standing behind Flash, pointed at me. "That bitch killed Morgan." Justin turned on his new partner. "How could you let her in?"

He didn't wait for an answer. Justin stalked over and shook his fist in my face. "You dare to show your face here? After what you did? Why aren't you in jail where you belong?"

No more. He'd made one accusation too many.

"Look, Justin. For the last time, I didn't kill Morgan. You have no right to blame me, so shut up or I'll bring a defamation suit. A big one."

He opened and closed his mouth but remained silent.

"Why aren't you blaming one of the women Morgan had an affair with? You know, someone like Flash over there. They had a lot more reason to kill your partner than I did."

Sadness and what looked like regret flickered over Justin's face. His shoulders fell. Again, I felt an unwanted sympathy for him. I lowered my voice. "We're hoping the police find the killer so we can all put this to rest." I softened my tone. "Do you know of anyone who would have done this to your friend?"

I'm not sure how I did it, but I set Justin off again.

He glared at me but spoke to Flash. "Get her out of my sight." Justin walked into the practice room, shoulders shaking. We could hear his sobs and Flash tearing up Ginger's application as we left.

We clattered down the stairs as if a bad witch—or Flash—chased us. We paused at the bottom of the stairs to catch our breath. Okay, so I could rest. Ginger's breathing stayed even. The sun shone bright and hot when we exited the building.

"Ginger, Justin is wearing a watch that looks like Morgan's."

"How do you know that?"

"I saw Morgan when I did CPR, and the one Justin wore looked the same."

My friend's face showed her disappointment. She

did that really well, probably from her years of practice with me.

"What? I want to know why anyone would pay so much for a watch." My high school Timex kept ticking, and that was good enough for me. "I don't get it. They aren't all that fancy looking."

"It's what's on the inside that counts." She wiggled her eyebrows at me. "Besides, he could have one of his own if what Mona said about Justin being the money man is right."

"It's white gold."

Ginger tsked.

"And I'm no expert, but Flash was wearing a vivid red lipstick."

"So?"

"It looked like the color used on my refrigerator."

Ginger's eyes narrowed into slits. I quickly remembered I hadn't told her about my last crisis. We headed to Dora's Cafe and I filled her in.

"That's it. You're staying with me and we'll use that damned security system Rob insisted on installing."

I made nasty eyes. "Ginger, don't tell me you've been in that house alone and not used the system." I threw my napkin over my unfinished hamburger. "That's it. I can see I have to take you in hand."

We smiled, finally at peace with each other again. I was glad to have her with me when we reached my house. I geared up to face my destroyed kitchen when a Get Solid crew truck pulled into my drive. Cam jumped down from the driver's side. The back truck doors opened and three more guys piled out.

"Cam, I'm sorry, but I can't help with the plans right now. How about I come in later and pound out the work?"

"Nah, forget it. Jim sent us over to help you clean up." His big hand dwarfed a shiny new house key on a tag I recognized. "Jim gave us the new key you left with him just in case you weren't here."

My chest hurt and I didn't know how to express myself. I settled for a gruff answer. "Well, come on in then, and let's see how bad it really is."

Ginger put her hand on Cam's arm. A quiet "thank you" floated to my ears. Some day I have to learn how to express myself better. Didn't look like it'd be soon, though, what with my plate filled with murder, blackmail and general mayhem. When I walked into the kitchen, my vocabulary remained limited. "Crap. Damn it. Crap."

The broken crockery was bad enough, but the Police Department's fingerprint powder desecrated my haven even more. I felt as if I'd stepped in rapid hardening cement. Ginger put her arm around my shoulders.

Cam looked at the refrigerator, eyes wide, and whistled. "Shit, Katie."

Ginger dropped her arm and clapped her hands. "All right, guys, let's get moving." She addressed Cam. "Do you have shovels in the truck? Garbage bins? What about wipe rags?"

Cam tore his gaze from the lipstick message. "Yeah, come on, let's get started." The crew left, unusually silent but for their heavy footsteps.

Ginger pulled me into a hug and patted my back. "We'll make it right, Katie. You'll see."

Tears welled up in my eyes. I don't cry often, but the sight of my kitchen on top of the last week or so, had me primed. "Why? Who could hate me this much?"

My friend's gaze took in the kitchen. "I'm not so sure it's about you."

The crew stomped in and we got going. Ginger's cryptic statement kept my brain occupied while we cleaned. Most of my stuff was vintage Goodwill, so no great loss. I eyed the Fiesta Ware and Manhattan Glass. Why were those pieces spared? Was it done deliberately? Did the intruder run out of time? I mulled that along with Ginger's observation and before I knew it, the kitchen had undergone a major cleanup. I'd have to stock up on paper plates until I could hit some yard sales or Goodwill, but otherwise, everything looked good.

Ginger cleaned the message off the fridge door as best she could, but a residue remained. That must have been some kinda strong cosmetic.

"Thanks, guys, I owe you one."

Cam threw his arm over my shoulders. "Don't worry about it, Katie. Just get past this and come back, okay? Jim is messing up the plans real bad." He clapped his hand over his mouth. "But don't say I said that, huh? And take your time if you're not feeling up to coming back right away."

A grin stole across my face. "Don't worry. I'll make it in tomorrow and I'll bring the doughnuts and coffee."

Cam's relieved look made my smile grow. "Thanks, Katie, and I hope they find this guy."

I punched his shoulder to keep from tearing up. "Me too."

After the crew left, Ginger and I made sure the doors and windows were secure. She helped me pack enough stuff for a week. I trusted Dirk and Matt would find the creep threatening Ginger and me before then.

As we drove away, I looked back at my bungalow. I hoped it stood in one piece when I returned. Turning to the front, I asked, "Ginger, can you help me pick out some lipstick?"

She stood on the brakes and I almost hit the windshield. "Lipstick? For you?" Ginger hit the gas and gave me a speculative look. "Honey, Dirk has it bad for you. You don't need cosmetics to draw him in." My friend returned her attention to the road. "Unless you want to make a slavering idiot out of him." She paused. "You may want to wait until he catches the bad guy before you do that."

"Oh for cripes sake. I'm wondering about the lipstick on my fridge."

Ginger sighed. "I was afraid of that."

"What does that crack mean?"

"Never mind. You're probably wondering what kind of lipstick comes in that shade, right?"

"Right."

"An expensive tube. I'm pretty sure that shade was in last year's spring line."

I pulled out Dirk's business card. The back was smeared with a sample from my fridge. "You up for a trip to Nordstrom's?"

Ginger didn't answer, just made the turn leading to Charlotte and the closest mall. Friends don't let friends go to cosmetic counters alone.

****

I opened Ginger's door to let Dirk and Matt enter. Dirk fired an opening salvo before I could greet them. "What the hell were you thinking?"

"I'm thinking those words are the only way you

162

know how to say hello to me."

Dirk ran his hands through his unevenly cut hair. I wished he'd let me do that for him, but then he couldn't display his frustration. With me.

"I can't believe you waltzed into the Yoga Studio and asked two possible suspects questions. I did get that right, didn't I?"

Gulp. "Um, yes? Flash is a suspect?"

"I'm the one asking questions. Did you or didn't you go to the Yoga Studio today?"

I bobbled my head.

"Did you get into an altercation with Justin Nash?"

Ginger walked up behind me. "It wasn't an altercation. More of he shouted and she tried to calm him down."

Dirk tapped his fingers on the doorframe. "Oh, really?"

I winced at his sarcastic tone. A quick glance at Matt's impassive expression told me that didn't go down well. Not well at all.

He slapped the frame with the palm of his hand. "I've got a witness who says Katie started it and kept it up after Justin walked away."

"Flash. That bitch."

He narrowed his gaze at me. "Funny, that's what she said about you." He massaged his chin. "Used the same tone."

"Why the hell aren't you arresting Flash? She has motive and opportunity, more than me. And she keeps trying to pin this murder on me. I vote for Flash."

"We're looking at a number of suspects."

He fixed Ginger with his Official Cop Look. "I'd like to discuss your visit to the Yoga Studio. May we come in, Mrs. Howe?"

They walked to the living room, me at the rear. "Ms. Sheridan, this interview is with Mrs. Howe."

Matt shook his head at me, and I got the message. Don't push it.

I took refuge in the kitchen and pulled out the ingredients for oatmeal-chocolate chip-raisin-nut cookies. Ginger named them "kitchen sink" cookies. I called them comfort food.

I was performing a cookie dough taste test when Matt walked in.

"Hey, Katie. That batter looks good."

"As an opening line, it's better than the one your partner used on me earlier."

"Yeah, he's frustrated." Matt parked his butt on a stool at the counter. He accepted my offer of ice tea and wiped his finger through the condensation.

"Katie, Dirk told me about your fight."

"I thought guys didn't discuss stuff like that."

He curled his lips down and snorted. "We don't, but when my partner acted like a short-tempered shit all day, I offered to beat it out of him."

I dropped my dough tasting spoon into the mixing bowl. "He what?"

"The guy is worried about you." He gulped tea. "I have to say, I am too."

"Why? I'm here with Ginger. We have an alarm system and soon we'll have cookies. We're good."

"Not so good." He watched his tea but it didn't move. Neither did his gaze. "Our boss isn't so sure you're a victim."

"What? You're joking, right?" I took a deep breath. "What about the mess in my kitchen?"

"He thinks you could have set that up."

"The attempted hit and run?"

"Didn't happen that way. You lost control of the bike."

"The BM? The shots fired?"

"BM? Oh, blackmailer. You could be in cahoots with someone or hired the job out."

"Hired the job out? What, was he kidding? I work as a drafter. My salary wouldn't let me hire out...a babysitter. Not that I need one. I thought he'd given up on me as the poisoner."

"Someone with official pull is demanding he take another look."

"Flash, that bitch." Thinking back, I remembered she'd been chummy with the mayor's wife at class that morning. "The mayor."

"Bingo. When we interviewed Ms. Wells, she said her affair with Anderson ended amicably. The man's business partner backed her up about the affair. Said he knew Anderson and Ms. Wells were friendly."

"Of course he said that. She's his new partner. He needs her cash."

Matt leaned across the counter and enclosed my shaking hand. "Katie we're watching out for you. You won't get railroaded on our watch."

"Thanks, Matt." I took a deep breath. "Can you tell me if you're looking at Rob Howe?"

He hesitated. "We're working the case, Katie. You know that's all I can say." Matt put his hand on my shoulder. "Don't worry and let us do our job. Everything will work out."

Dirk's voice sounded from the doorway. "You better check whatever you've got in the oven."

165

I turned and saw wisps of smoke curling up from the stove vents. "Damn, I hate when that happens." I pulled the test batch cookie sheet from the oven. A little judicious scraping may have made the cookies edible, but I wasn't up to the task.

"Matt, let's go." Brr. Dirk's tone would have been handy in an August heat wave.

Matt shrugged, winked and squeezed my hand. He met Dirk at the door and answered his glare. "What? You told me to get her story."

Dirk glared and left without a backward glance. Matt followed after a quick wave in my direction.

Ginger opened the back door and turned on the kitchen fan. "Boy, Howdie, girl. Whatever you're doing, keep it up. That man is hot for you."

"Yeah, and I'm in hot water. Again." I looked between the cookie dough and Ginger. "Should we just eat it raw or bake it? I vote for dough fest."

She removed the mitts from my hand and moved me to the stool Matt had occupied. "Sit. Tell me all about it." Ginger found two clean cookie sheets and started filling them. "Can you start water for tea? In about fifteen minutes, we'll each have a dozen cookies straight from the oven. We'll need something liquid to help us drown our sorrow."

Chapter Sixteen

I was deep in my work when the phone rang. I snagged the receiver without looking away from my computer screen.

"Rob's back." Ginger's voice sounded calm, but I could about feel her shaking through the phone line.

I wondered if the BM would send Ginger another note with Rob back in town. If that happened, the coincidence would be too much for Ginger to ignore. Crap. I hoped for his innocence, even if he had acted like a shit lately.

"So did he tell you where he was for the past couple of days?"

"I didn't ask and I'm not so sure I care."

Whoa. Ginger's tone made me wonder if she spoke in front of Rob. If she had, he would have had no illusions about her feelings.

She continued, "He finally admitted he lost our money in a high-risk investment, but that's not what has me pissed."

I knew Rob must be in the room with her. "What does?"

"Rob's inability to communicate."

The obvious answer to give Ginger was that her using me as a middleman to their conversation wasn't exactly communicating either. But something held me back. Maybe it was my belief she needed to vent. My reticence didn't last long. "Ginger, you should be saying this to Rob, not me."

"I know. But I'm too angry to look him in the eye, much less talk without screaming."

"You're doing a great job of it with me. Just transfer your vent to him."

"Oh, all right." She hung up and I mirrored the action.

A shadow fell over my papers. I looked up and saw Dirk and Matt stood in front of me. Crap. Either they were in Ninja mode or I'd lost my hearing because I hadn't noticed the Get Solid trailer door open. If I'd heard them coming, I would've been hiding in the bathroom instead of wanting to cower under my desk.

Dirk's jaw looked tight but he managed to comment. "I take it Rob Howe returned."

"Um, yeah. He's back."

They had that cop partner thing happening. Without either of them speaking, Matt pulled out his phone and made a call to the station. I could hear him because Dirk didn't talk, just glared.

"I'm not talking to you, Johnson. If you have questions, Detective Pulaski can ask them. He knows how to be nice to me." I sniffed. "At least he says hello when we meet, not like some people I know."

He rubbed his hand through his hair. My attention followed the furrows his fingers left in his do. Simultaneously, his silent treatment bugged me.

"You here to arrest me? Because if you are, I finally have the name of a lawyer I can call."

Dirk frowned. "No, we're not here to arrest you. Feeling guilty?"

Matt ended his call. "We came to ask if Mrs. Howe

had gotten another blackmail note." He looked at Dirk, but whatever he saw made him continue instead of turning over the conversational ball. "There haven't been any calls to your home, so we figured you've been okay."

"I've been at Ginger's." With Rob back, I'd be returning to my bungalow. The unhappy couple needed time alone. Ginger's anger wouldn't preclude her listening to his story and letting him stay there. At least overnight.

Dirk's expression darkened. It seemed he could hear my thoughts and didn't like them. "Where will you be tonight?"

I played with the idea of not telling him for about ten seconds. "At home."

They exchanged cop looks. Crap. I hated when they did that.

Dirk tilted his head to the side. "That's not a good idea."

Matt quietly backed away. "Mind if I use the john?"

I pointed down the hall. "Go ahead, Matt."

Neither of us said anything until he left the room. Even then the silence drew tight. Dirk broke it. "Look, I'm sorry if I stepped on your toes but—"

"Stepped on my toes? I don't think so." I searched for the right words, an elegant phrase. "Stomped 'em is what you did." I didn't wait for him to find an excuse. "Either you trust me and think I'm innocent or you don't. Make up your mind and stop jerking my chain."

"He trusts you and we both know you're innocent. Johnson can't help himself. He's a dip shit." Matt's response made me jump because I didn't hear him return. Gotta get my ears checked.

Dirk snorted.

Matt threw his hands up, palm outward. "What, you got a problem with that, partner?"

Cop Sexy A-hole ran his hand through his hair again. Maybe he did that regular scalp massage to keep his mop head healthy. Could be it had nothing to do with frustration. Then again, probably not.

He sighed. "Yes, Katie, I think you're innocent. I believe you and have from the first. We've got to check out everyone's alibis and stories. You just happen to have a well-connected enemy." He placed his index finger against his lips. "Are you sure you don't know our boss?"

"I appreciate you two stopping by, but I'm on deadline here. Ask me your questions or tell me what you came here to say, then you'll have to leave."

Matt rubbed his lips and I knew he wiped off a smile. I could see the corners of his mouth tilted up. My lips twitched in sympathetic response. "Johnson, ask her already."

My breath halted in my chest. Ask me what?

"Do you know where Rob Howe has been?"

Disappointment made my voice curt. "No, you'll have to ask him."

"We will, but we were hoping you could give us some facts to check his story against."

That was such bull. They were on the way here before Ginger called. Overhearing my conversation with her was pure accident. I narrowed my eyes at Dirk, and once again, he read my thoughts perfectly. Maybe my small growl helped his interpretation.

"Christ. All right all ready. I came to apologize and

to see how you're doing, okay?" He gave Matt's shoulder a light punch. "Did I say it good enough for you?"

Matt laughed. "You should ask Katie, not me."

I had my arms crossed and a stern look on my face.

"Katie, I wanted to ask, well, I hoped that you..." His words stumbled dead. He took a deep breath. "I just need to know you're doing okay, that's all."

Matt shook his head. "My partner is a wimp. How did I get so lucky?"

Dirk ran his hand through his hair once more then pushed past Matt. The door swung shut behind him.

I looked to Matt. "What the heck was that about?"

His mouth dropped open. "I can't believe you don't know." He shut his mouth and his gaze searched mine. "You two are a mess."

He walked out before I could process Matt's parting shot.

****

"Katie. I found another blackmail note. It was in an envelope on the front stoop."

"I don't believe it."

Minutes later I held irrefutable proof. Ginger had gotten another BM note. It appeared the same as the others, with cut out words from magazines and newspapers. Maybe we should have alerted the recycle crew to look for mutilated magazines in the neighborhood bins. Not that this creep recycled. He didn't seem the responsible type.

My attention returned to the note.

Last chance. Leave money at Kannapolis train station's lost and found for Jim Jones at 10:15 tonight. No cops. Mess up and your husband and friend die.

Holy Crap. "Ginger, did you tell Rob what I said in the cemetery? Her confused look was my answer. "You know, about having to traipse through the dark instead of leaving the bag at the train station?"

"No. We haven't talked about the blackmail. I hoped to keep it from him, remember? Although why I bothered is beyond me now."

"Maybe the BM heard me bitching and decided to steal the idea." That bit of reasoning didn't settle my stomach. "We'd better get the money case from wherever you stashed it and prepare for the drop off."

"I can't."

My stomach tied itself into knots. The conversation wasn't headed in a direction I wanted to follow. "What do you mean, you can't?"

"The police have the money."

My head spun. "What? They what?"

"Evidence." She gulped. "Dirk said he was keeping the bag as evidence because a crime was committed."

Now in addition to a macramé stomach and spinning head, I had a tight jaw. Dirk had pulled more of his "gotta keep the little women safe" crap. "We didn't commit a crime. Well, except for trespassing on private property. And destroying some of the flower arrangements, but I went back and paid for those the next day."

"He tacked on cemetery desecration."

"Oh, that's such baloney." My foot tapped a jig but I didn't feel like dancing.

"Sandwich meat or not, they kept the bag."

"I hope you got a receipt for it. I've heard too many stories about stuff disappearing from locked evidence rooms." Crap. Now we'd have to tell Dirk and

Matt about the note.

"What's that you're mumbling, Katie?"

"We'll have to go to the police."

She leveled a look that made me hunch my shoulders. "Pardon me? You were the one insisting we tell them as soon as a note came. What're you thinking?" Now Ginger parroted Dirk's refrain.

I inhaled the biggest breath I could pull into my lungs. "I really don't want to say this to you."

Ginger waited patiently and I couldn't see a way to avoid relating my dark thoughts. "I thought, in case the BM is someone you know, you may want to deliver the money yourself."

Her flat response fired back. "It's not Rob."

My dry throat didn't loosen after attempting some swallows. "We don't know that."

Ginger caught my hands "It's not Rob. He's a screw-up and lately he's been a total jerk, but he's not a murderer. Whoever was in the cemetery at the last drop wanted to kill us. That's not Rob."

I could feel the truth loosen my stomach muscles. "You're right."

"Whoever shot at us is a cold person, calculating. Maybe angry."

I raised my hand. "I vote for Flash."

Ginger smiled. "You aren't giving up on that line, are you?"

"Nope." I moved to envelope Ginger in a hug. "I'll let you call Dirk."

She stepped away from me but her gaze imitated an x-ray. "What did you do now?" She planted her palms against her hips. "Katie Sheridan. Don't you dare tell me you let Cop Sexy get away."

"Okay, I won't."

Ginger wanted to jump on my response like a hot-streak batter on a fastball pitch, but I found salvation. Rob walked in just as she wound up for the strike. My friend slid the blackmail note behind her back and into her waistband.

He looked like crap and that was a generous assessment. "Hi, girls. What's up?"

Ginger's pleading look got me talking too fast. "I stayed with Ginger because my house got messed up so I came to get my clothes because I won't be staying now that you're home not that I don't like you but my kitchen is clean so thanks and gotta run." I turned and hurried for the guest room.

Even though I brought enough for a week, most of my clothes were tees and jeans. I had only two bags to fill, and the packing didn't take long. I crept into the kitchen and saw Rob leaving. She pulled the note from her waistband and shoved it at me.

"You'll have to give this to Dirk."

I pushed it back toward her. "It's your note. You do it."

Chicken squawks were her answer.

"Talk about chicken...what about Rob?"

"I've decided it's time to have it out with him. That's my priority. The police will handle the money drop off tonight. It doesn't matter who delivers the note to them." She clucked and flapped her arms.

"Call Matt if you're determined to avoid Dirk." She turned away then swung back. "You've got to trust a man, soon. He's a good guy, Katie."

Crap. I never thought Ginger would literally turn on me, but she was right. I could call Matt and report the note. It was four o'clock, past time to get on it. They'd need enough notice to set up their operation.

I searched my purse but couldn't find Matt's card. Dirk's was there, but I didn't need to look at the number. I had it memorized. How's that for juvenile?

He picked up on the second ring. "Detective Johnson."

His deep voice stopped my breath, but it started again after a two seconds. Good thing. Blue face isn't the best look for me. "It's me. Ginger got another note." My voice shook as I read it to him.

"You okay?"

I forced a smile so my voice sounded perky. "Sure. Just great." No way would he know my shakes came from talking to him, not because of the note. "I'll let you go. The BM isn't giving you much time. You'll have to get your team together."

"Katie, I...um." He fell silent and I moved to hang up when he sighed. "I care about you, uh, your safety. And I'll need to see the note."

My throat tightened. "Sure, Dirk."

"And keep the damn doors locked. Your car and your house."

"I'm not six years old."

He didn't answer right away and my blood heated toward boil. When it came, his low voiced reply hit my solar plexus. "It's a good thing you're not six. Yep, a really good thing." He paused. His voice lowered to a whisper. "You know that little black number you wore the other night?"

A shiver hit the back of my neck. I'd say. My body clearly remembered the scrape of his teeth as he removed it. I wiggled in my chair and held the receiver closer to my ear.

His regular voice hit my ear. I jumped. "Yes, sir. Another note arrived this afternoon. I'm arranging to pick it up right now."

Whoa. Dirk's official voice talking to his superior crashed my sexual haze. Our game playing wasn't appropriate, not even if he used my own sexuality against me to keep me safe. I wasn't sure our budding relationship was more than a game to Dirk. He had some serious memories cramping him. Well, so did I.

He finished his other conversation. "Now where were we?"

"Dirk, I have to run an errand in your direction. I can drop the note off with the Desk Sergeant."

His voice dropped to a murmur. Obviously his boss had gone but someone else was near. "If I pick up the note, I get to see you."

Instead of inflaming me, now his sexy whisper pissed me off. "I don't think that's a good idea. Ginger doesn't need the cops coming to her house again. If the BM is watching, it'll look like she's called you in."

"Come on, Katie. Give me a break. I can be discreet."

"I'll bring the note to you. It'll take me about half an hour." It'd be there in half the time because no way did I want to see Dirk lounging casually at the front desk. "We can talk after the case is closed."

I hung up. Crap. So much for trust.

Chapter Seventeen

Avoiding Dirk was easy. Concentrating when I knew what would go down later that evening wasn't. After dropping off the note, I headed for the Get Solid trailer. I felt some trepidation about going in, but my desk was clear when I arrived. Jim probably didn't want to hear my screeching, not that he graced the trailer with his presence.

I settled down and checked the notes piled neatly on my desk. Cam had been there. I recognized his organizational style. After making a note to send him an engagement gift—a twelve pack of his favorite micro-brewery beers—I got down to it.

Supervisors greeted me as they returned from their jobs. Phew. I'd been able to hide from my problems for a few hours.

Everyone left and my stomach growled. I reached Dora's Café in record time. I ordered, sipped my water and waited for supper. Dora set my cheeseburger platter down.

"Dora, you make a cheeseburger platter like no one else in the world. Yum."

"You ain't tasted it yet."

"Anticipation based on past history. Got any ketchup? This bottle's empty."

Allen nabbed the stool next to mine. "Speaking of anticipation, when are you and Dirk going to get together? I could use some new shoes." He clamped his mouth shut and looked away.

"You've got a pool going? On when Dirk and I will get together?"

Dora arrived with the ketchup. "Honey, they ain't the only ones."

My mouth felt wired shut but I managed to speak. "You're losers. Both of you. All of the people in the pool. What's wrong with this town that your only entertainment is whether and when I get laid?"

Dora and Allen exchanged looks. Dora pursed her mouth. "You thinking what I'm thinking?"

Allen drawled his answer. "Yep. Sounds like a done deed to me."

Dora leaned against her counter. "Guess you'll need to change the bet."

Allen played with a napkin. "How about the date they go public?"

"What kinda odds you givin'?"

Allen gave me a long look. I could feel my face heat under his regard. "Hey, you two I'm sitting right here."

Dora pushed the ketchup bottle to me. I squeezed and a quarter bottle of condiment hit my burger. I kept my head down and used my knife to scrape the excess ketchup to the side. The stuff came out so fast Dora couldn't be using a name brand, no matter what the bottle label claimed. "Forget the pool. We're not a couple."

Allen chuckled. "I'd say the odds just changed."

"A lot you know." I kept my head down and shoveled in fries so I couldn't say more.

Dora tipped her head to the side. I could feel her

stare.

Allen tapped his fingers against the counter. "I could still use a new pair of shoes."

They both eyed me.

Dora turned to the register and rummaged for paper and pen. She scribbled something and pulled a crumpled fiver out of her pocket. The café owner handed both to Allen. "Maybe you need shoes, but my coffeepots are old."

Crumbs flew out of my mouth at her statement. Dora ran a steady goldmine.

Allen grasped my shoulder. "Listen, Katie. I have a message for you from Dirk."

"I should care, why?"

Allen rolled his eyes. "You're pushing it girl."

Dora chimed in. "Maybe I should rethink my bet." She saw Allen's look and moved off.

Allen lowered his voice and followed Dora's progress before speaking. "Dirk insists you stay out of Kannapolis tonight." He correctly read my mutinous look. "He's not kidding. You need to stay away. These things are never a sure thing, even with the best planning."

"I never said I would show up."

Allen rolled his eyes. I really had to rethink small-town living.

"Look, Katie, everyone at the station knows he's crazy about you."

"News to me."

"You can fight your attraction all you want, but we all see it. You always were a stubborn little thing." He crossed his arms across his chest. "Promise me you won't show tonight. Dirk will have my head otherwise."

"Scared to ask me, is he? Not that he asks. He's more the ordering around type."

"He's the team leader and up to his neck in logistical planning. It says a lot that he asked me to find you and get your promise. He thinks it's so he can stop worrying but I know Dirk. A part of him will keep hoping you're safe, even when he's throwing handcuffs on the perp. Get it now?"

The stool didn't feel stable so I grasped the counter edge. Allen's words pointed to an involvement my insecurities didn't want to accept. The backs of my eyes burned. I swallowed hard. "But I thought he, well, you know. I'm a substitute for his partner, Amy. "

Allen sighed. "Amy was his partner, not his girlfriend. Contrary to television, if we're lucky, we draw a partner who becomes a friend. We don't screw them, not in any way, shape or form. Not a smart move."

"Oh."

"So do you get it now? And keep your nose and the rest of you out of Kannapolis."

I wasn't a person who listened to police scanners or rubbernecked accidents. I hadn't considered being anywhere near the bust. I didn't know how I felt about being on the scene. Part of me thought it a really dumb idea and another part thought revenge on the BM a dish best served hot.

Allen waited.

"Okay. I'll keep a distance between me and tonight's bust."

His forehead creased. My answer hadn't soothed his soul. He opened his mouth then closed it. Cocking his head, he found what he wanted to see in my face. "Thanks, Katie."

Allen stood and called to the café owner on his way out. "Take it easy, Dora. Don't buy those coffee pots just yet. I think I've got new shoes in my future."

Dora sang under her breath while she thumbed through a gossip magazine at the other end of the counter. If nothing else, the two bet-taking gamblers had kept my mind off tonight's main event for a few minutes. I paid my bill and walked outside.

My phone rang. I hesitated answering, seeing as the dang thing brought me nothing but bad news. I snapped it open, hoping I'd hear something good for a change.

A muffled voice responded to my greeting.

"Make the drop-off tonight or your friend dies."

I didn't have time to think about the message much less answer it. The BM hung up.

The evening had turned cool and clear. Perfect weather for relaxing on the porch, committing a crime, or driving to neighboring Kannapolis. It didn't take long to make my decision.

****

Kannapolis is a cute little town, all old buildings and new buildings made to look old. The train station is one of the latter, all red brick, including the sidewalks. Usually it's a middling busy place, but tonight the place jumped with people and action. All the spaces were filled with cars. Adults talked with each other or stood at the iron fence, gazing down the tracks.

Okay, maybe I should have called Dirk and stayed home behind locked doors, but sitting in Ginger's loaner car at the Kannapolis train station parking lot seemed safe. My friend wanted to come with me, but she'd already made plans with Rob. I'd settled for bringing her car instead. One of us had to be here in case the BM watched. After that phone call, I wouldn't take a chance.

I slid down behind the wheel just in case Dirk was near. The man had some kind of Katie radar. The thing about radar is it worked both ways. My tingling skin worked as my own personal early warning system. Dirk was definitely in the area.

My watch read almost ten fifteen. One of the adults standing at the spike topped wrought iron fence pointed, and a train whistle sounded in the distance. People moved from the parking lot to the large open area in front of the station.

An older woman in an Amtrak uniform emerged from a side door and locked it behind her. She walked to the tall gate barring everyone from the train tracks. The woman unlocked the gate and pushed both sides open. She said something that kept everyone where they were, but the crowd's craning heads and shifting bodies portrayed excitement.

The engineer gave a few more blasts of the train whistle, whistle being a misnomer for sure. That sucker was loud. Cars rolled past the largish crowd of adults, and the engine huffed to a stop with the middle of the train at the gates. Doors on three or four of the cars slammed open. A conductor jumped off and pulled down the steps. Teenagers streamed off the train, backpacks slung over an arm, hurrying toward waiting parents.

I averted my eyes from the warm homecoming and returned my attention to the small terminal. Crafty BM.

The bag had been turned in to lost and found and now the desk was unattended with the Station Master outside. The woman had gotten tied up getting dozens of passengers and their band equipment offloaded so the train's schedule wasn't blown. Depending upon how Dirk's team played it, the BM could waltz in and dance out with the bag undetected.

A man carrying a familiar bag came around the building's corner. Damn. A ball cap jammed down his hair, but I knew that muscular chest. Justin.

I gaped. That's all I could do. I had no time to reason why Justin as the bad guy made little sense.

Dirk stepped from the back of the building while Matt and four other officers detached from the crowd of parents and teens to circle Justin. No one moved too close, maybe because they didn't know if Justin came armed.

My heart pumped with sympathetic adrenaline. I watched Dirk speak to Justin and motioned for him to drop the bag. Justin's body geared to run when he looked around and saw the cops behind him. He dropped the bag and his shoulders.

The police were focused on making a safe bust and they didn't notice two parents pushing a cart full of band equipment toward them. I anticipated the problem a split second before Dirk. He called an order to the officers to keep the crowd away. Cop Bossy was too late.

Justin got into a crouch, looking like he'd drop to the ground. He never flattened. Instead, he used the crouch like a linebacker. Two of the officers who could have stopped Justin had turned away to deal with the oncoming parents.

He didn't hesitate. Justin's shoulder hit Dirk in the gut. Dirk got pushed into another cop and both landed on their butts on the brick sidewalk. Justin took off and dived behind the wheel of a car with the engine running. Wheels squealed and he was gone.

Undercover cops ran for nearby cars. Two patrol cruisers took off, sirens and lights strobing.

I breathed a sigh of relief. Dirk was safe. No one had gotten seriously hurt and Justin didn't get Ginger's money. It could have been much worse.

****

Dirk limped to my car and rapped on the window, his knock an unvoiced order. I tried my underutilized sympathy gene on him. "You look sore. Did landing on the brick sidewalk hurt much?"

"That's not what burns my butt." His glare charred my retinas. "What the hell are you thinking, Katie? You're not supposed to be here. You could be tagged as an accomplice."

My mouth needed saliva. I gulped. "But I haven't even talked to Justin."

His lips twisted in what I could only interpret as disgust. Uh oh. "Yeah, and you couldn't have made arrangements beforehand?" He swiped his hand through his chopped hair. "My boss is gonna have a field day with this." His head dropped and I almost didn't hear his mutter. "If I keep my job."

"What's the problem? Justin won't get away. You've got the money and you can place him at the scene. He'll go away for a long time, right?"

He shook his head. "Amtrak officials only said they had a full train. We didn't have time to check out the number of passengers getting off here." He looked at the terminal. "I thought we had it covered."

"Stuff happens."

"This was my bust. It was my decision to go, even with the crowd. We should have backed off."

But Dirk hadn't backed off. My stomach churned. I had a strong idea he wanted this bust because he worried the BM would come after me, or Ginger. Dating a cop, no matter how hot, had a downside. If we got together, I wouldn't be free to do stupid stuff. My actions would directly affect him. That's way too much responsibility for someone who can't handle a cat or dog. Or even a plant.

"Dirk, I'm sorry I came here. Sorry I keep making dumb mistakes, but it's not your fault the bust went bad. Justin had information you didn't. You'll catch him."

His stricken look didn't reassure me. "My miscalculation killed Amy. It could have been worse tonight." He put his hand on my car roof and leaned closer, but not for a kiss. "Go home, Katie." He walked away.

My chest tightened. I sat for a minute to clear my blurred vision then started the car and drove off. Matt and Allen talked at the driveway's entrance. When they spotted me, their disappointed looks grabbed my chest and blurred my vision all over again. I managed to drive away without crashing.

The night's events sucked. My fling with Dirk ended before it started. I reached for my cell phone but remembered Ginger had her hands full dealing with Rob. That left home. Damn it. It still felt unsafe, but better than a hotel. And since I knew who the blackmailer was, he wasn't likely to try to blow my house down.

I pulled in the drive and saw a momentary flash in the dense bushes that line my drive. The flicker didn't repeat, even when I flipped my headlights to high beam. I grabbed my flashlight but it didn't flick on. Damn it, forgot to change the batteries. My gut reaction told me to go back to Ginger's, but I didn't listen. Instead, I decided to put on my big girl pants and suck it up.

Headlights off? Check.

Pepper spray in hand? I fumbled in the bottom of my purse. Check.

Car keys between the fingers of my other hand? Check.

Now how the hell did I leave the car with both hands full? Transferring the spray to the other hand, I started to get out and then decided to flip my headlights back on. Better a dead battery than dead.

A big inhalation and I left the car and ran for the front porch. My right foot hovered above the bottom step when someone tackled me from behind. I jerked my head to the side, avoiding cracking it open on the stairs, but a hand at my throat made me think unconsciousness preferable to what I faced. Justin.

Spittle sprayed my face. "Bitch."

I looked into his dilated pupils and knew I'd die unless I did something to save myself. And then he'd go after Ginger.

"You killed Morgan and you won't get away with it."

If I could shake my head I would have, but he had me pinned down. A sound that resembled "no" made its way from my throat.

"Give it up, slut. You killed him because he wouldn't sleep with you. A friend told me." Justin's tears hit my cheeks. "You didn't try to save him. If someone else could have gotten close, he'd still be alive today."

Pressure from his hands increased and my air supply dwindled. No time left. I worked my hand with the pepper spray free and pointed the nozzle toward him, hoping it hit the bastard in the face.

Bingo. I heard his scream and the pressure loosened. I sucked in air just before he bore down again. My vision turned to gray. Justin must have thought he finished the job because he removed his hands. The pressure on my chest disappeared. I blacked out.

****

"Katie, are you okay? Katie. Do you hear me? Katie?"

A familiar voice called me. My throat burned and I moved my hand to it. Heavy arms made that simple task impossible. One hand fell near my nose and the smell on my fingers made me nauseous. Pepper spray.

My eyelids rose but my vision remained blurred. Tears leaked from my eyes, falling to my cheeks. A large gray mass stood suspended above me. Justin. I had to get away before he saw I wasn't dead.

I rolled to my side and attempted to rise but I was pushed onto my back. "Nooo." My voice sounded like nothing more than a croak but I knew I had to persuade Justin to not kill me. "Let me 'splain. Didn't kill Morgan."

A large hand pushed a tangle of hair from my face. "Calm down, Katie. It's Allen." I felt a rough square of cloth dry my cheeks.

"Justin..." My voice gave out and my eyes fluttered shut.

"Relax. We've got him."

Bright red lights appeared and disappeared against my eyelids. Allen called out. "Hey, over here! Bring the gurney. Move it!"

Chapter Eighteen

Clattering echoed in my ears. My nose twitched with an odor that was one part floral and two parts astringent. I had to be at the Northeast Medical Center. No other place sounded or smelled like this, not to mention I'd been here too many times not to recognize it in my sleep. I cracked my eyelids and checked out my location from under eyelashes. The cardboard art in plastic frames and the fact that I lay flat on my back confirmed it. I never slept on my back. I didn't hook myself up to IV drips, either.

Exhausted from the covert room assessment, my eyes drifted closed. Too late. My surveillance had been spotted.

"Katie? You awake?

Ginger. Even if I hadn't recognized her voice, I would have known the scent , the essential oils she used to protect against viruses. Smart girl, wearing the oils here. She sat on the edge of her chair almost close enough to share my bed.

Dirk's spicy tang hit my sensory system. Licking my lips when he came near was a knee-jerk reaction. Too bad my dry tongue wiped dry lips. It felt like sandpaper on charcoal.

"Water." Yeuw. That croak sounded worse than awful.

Ginger held an industrial sized-water container and

guided the straw to my mouth. In my funk, I'd expected icy cold water but got lukewarm chlorinated crap. The sucked lemon expression I flashed Ginger encouraged her to withdraw the container. The water I spit back into the cup spurted onto my hospital gown and dribbled down my chin.

Ginger stepped back. Her eyes and mouth were wide, her face pale. "I'm so sorry. Here, let me clean up the mess."

She pulled at a tissue box programmed to release only one thin sheet at a time. Dirk reached across me and grabbed the box. He ripped it open, and a block of tissue fell on my chest. My visitors shared a look over my head. "I'll get this. Why don't you see if the nurse will give you some fresh water with ice?" He studied my garb. "And a dry gown."

Ginger nodded and hurried from the room. If I hadn't felt so punk, I'd enjoy the care Dirk took with the tissues and my wet chest. Who says hospital wear isn't sexy?

"What happened?" The spit of water I swallowed hadn't improved my death rattle.

Dirk's hand paused. He tossed a wad of wet tissue into a nearby trashcan. He didn't look at me and his voice was too casual. "What do you remember?"

It hurt to think but I concentrated. "Saw something. Bushes. Pepper spray."

Ginger returned and I took a long pull on the straw. Dirk jerked his head slightly, her cue to leave the room. She stayed with me. That's my BFF.

My throat felt better. I swirled a piece of ice into my mouth and sucked on it. "Got tackled from behind." My eyes closed against the memory, but my Mama didn't raise no sissy. "Justin. He tried to kill me."

The thought that he almost succeeded was not one I wanted to air. "That's all I know."

Ginger put the sweating water container on the bed tray and her hands on her hips. "Why is there a guard on the door? I almost didn't get back in here. A nurse had to vouch for me."

Dirk's guarded eyes and expressionless face made my stomach drop. "My boss ordered it."

I could see Ginger getting wound up for her semi-annual temper tantrum. Lately though, her anger level was almost as high as mine. "Is it for Katie's protection or is she under arrest?" Her foot tapping sounded loud in the sudden quiet.

Dirk pushed his fingers through his hair. Uh oh. Didn't think I'd like what came next. His gaze held an apology.

"My boss still wants to pin the murder on you." He shrugged but that didn't excuse the crap he'd just tossed at me. "He's kind of a one trick pony."

"No excuse. Justin ... tried to ... kill ... me. Would have gone ... after Ginger next." More water sluiced down my throat. I'd need a refill in a few minutes. "Blames me ... Morgan's death. Wants me...dead." I returned to the soothing safety of drinking ice water.

Ginger picked up the ball. "You boss isn't a one trick pony. He's an asshole." My friend had channeled me. She picked up my thoughts exactly, and in the tone and words I'd use. "Why?"

Dirk didn't play dumb. "My boss thinks the attempted murder is proof of a falling out between partners. He thinks Katie went to the station as backup."

Crap.

I'd thought I was in deep shit with Dirk. Ginger added another layer. "You were at the station? By yourself? What were you thinking? You told me you were reporting the last threat to the police. You promised you'd stay home."

Dirk smirked. I wished I could fake sleep, but knew that wouldn't work. Ginger had seen me do it too many times and Dirk's cop sense would pick it up in a nanosecond.

He crossed his arms. "I see I'm not the only person you hear that from."

Ginger stepped up to the plate and swung. "Get over yourself, buster. She's been my friend a long time. I have a right to first scold."

Dirk threw his hands up palm out and sat down. He crossed his legs and leaned back with his hands behind his head. "Go ahead. I'm going to enjoy this."

I stymied the reproach by holding up my IV'd hand. "I'm tired. Can you both leave? We'll discuss this later." My hand dropped to the blanket.

That request was no ruse. A spurt of energy had carried me only so far and would go no further. Ginger's gaze ran over my face, and whatever she saw convinced her I told the truth. That couldn't have been a good thing. My appearance, not my honesty.

"Wait. One thing." I looked at Dirk. "Have I told you what I think about your boss?"

"You sure you never dated him? He's got a big something against you."

"He's gonna be disappointed."

The last thing I saw before the backs of my eyelids were Dirk and Ginger's worried glances. Then I heard him say they'd posted a guard for my protection. That really couldn't be good.

****

The doctor said my throat would be sore for a while. Ginger wouldn't let me look in the mirror, not that I wanted to see the bruises Justin had likely given me. To take my mind off my pain, I asked her the main question bothering me.

"Ginger, why does Justin hate me so much?"

She looked up from her *Natural Foods* magazine. "I've been thinking about that while you slept. I think it's because you didn't save Morgan."

"Huh?"

She thumbed several pages then laid the magazine in her lap, meeting my gaze. "I think he was in love with Morgan. It's the only thing that makes sense."

I blinked. "Really?"

"Especially because he swears he isn't the murderer." She leaned her chin on her palm. "That and I used to catch Justin watching Morgan when he thought no one saw him. The poor man couldn't help himself."

"Do you think—"

"What?"

"Well, I wonder if Justin was one of Morgan's victims?"

"Probably. Morgan took Justin for a pile of money. The Yoga Studio set up shouldn't have cost the amount Justin said he paid in to the business. Morgan had to be taking money out of the partnership."

Poor Justin. Taken for a ride like one of Morgan's women.

"We know Justin picked up the blackmailing. He

admitted finding Morgan's records and photographs. He figured he should get a return on investment, I guess."

"But if he didn't kill Morgan, who put poison on the mat and block?"

"That's for me to discover. Don't even think about asking questions." Dirk's voice made my girl parts all squishy even as he ticked me off. Like I had a choice about being in the hospital.

His voice gentled. "Feeling any better?"

I nodded. "What's up with Justin? Ginger says he claims he didn't murder Morgan."

Dirk tossed a headshake Ginger's way then faced me. "I may as well tell you. You'll be bugging everyone for information otherwise." He pulled a chair closer to the bed and sat.

"The story starts over ten years ago." He paused. "Justin Nash played varsity football. Big Ten. I remembered him. Didn't get drafted but he was a solid player. Fast and tough."

I wouldn't know. SEC teams were the only ones I knew existed. But what happened to turn Justin from a tough athlete to a small business investor? Did I really want to know?

"Anderson and Nash attended the same college and developed a friendship. It's not clear if they stayed friends the entire time, but a few years ago, they hooked up again, right after Nash came into an inheritance. They formed a partnership and tried a few businesses, but nothing took until they started Yoga Studio."

Dirk leaned forward with his elbows on his knees. "Nash found out about the gifts and the blackmail. He'd lost most of his money to his business partner. With

Morgan out of the way, he decided to take over the scam."

I glanced at Ginger, proud she'd figured out much of the story for herself.

"Ginger thinks Justin hates me because I didn't save Morgan, but that doesn't make sense. Isn't Justin the murderer?"

Dirk hesitated before answering. "It's true Nash denies killing anyone, but that's no surprise. We can't place him at the cemetery for attempted homicide, and the gun used there hasn't been found. For my money, the combined blackmail, attempted murder charges won't put him away nearly long enough."

"Tack on malicious damage. I bet he's the one who broke into my house. And he stole Morgan's twenty-five thousand dollar watch. That's gotta be what, grand theft?" I decided not to mention the cemetery desecration, because Dirk didn't need a reminder about my part in that scene.

Dirk grinned. "Thanks, little Miss District Attorney. We'll check that out." His smile faded.

"You believe he's the murderer, don't you?"

Dirk clasped his hands and looked at the floor for a few moments. Then he caught my eye. "Could be."

Ginger piped up. "Why do you say that?"

Dirk's and my gazes held. "Just a gut feeling."

I knew about those. If I'd listened to the last big one I'd had, I wouldn't be lounging in this hard-assed hospital bed.

He looked at Ginger. "Nash told me Anderson said he wanted you to leave your husband. Run off together. Told Nash he planned to shut down the studio. They had a huge fight the night before the murder. What can you tell me about that?"

She grasped the arms of her chair. "Morgan asked me to elope, but I didn't believe him. I never took him seriously." She cleared her throat. "I had a fling, Detective Johnson, because my husband left me a little more day by day. I thought an affair would make me feel better. It didn't."

"Were you a blackmail victim of Anderson or Nash?" Dirk's kind tone and prudence got big marks from me.

"I didn't get a note until after Morgan died." She straightened in her chair. "But I have no doubt Morgan would have blackmailed me at some point. He had no conscience."

I reached over the bedside and she took my hand. "Oh, I don't know. That sounds like a strong motive to me. Justin's income gone and the man he worshipped taking off with a rich woman. And with a boatload of ill-gotten gains besides. It'd drive me to murder."

Dirk looked toward the door. "You may want to watch your words."

I rolled my eyes and avoided his stare. He turned his cop gaze toward Ginger. "Nash admits to calling your husband. I'd like to talk with you about that later."

Ginger paled. "We can speak now. I know about the call."

"So you know he revealed the affair, hoping to ruin your marriage in retaliation."'

A wave of confusion washed over me. "When was this? Why didn't you tell me, Ginger?"

"Rob finally brought it up the night Justin tried to kill you." She squeezed my fingers. "It was news to me too."

This raised a whole lot of questions I wouldn't ask in front of Dirk and with a too fuzzy brain. "Did Justin have a partner besides Morgan or did he pull all of this off on his own?"

"He lawyered up and we didn't get anything more."

Against my better judgment, I brought up a point that bothered me. "The destruction in my kitchen didn't seem to follow Justin's pattern. It had a sly feel to it. The stuff Justin did reminded me of, well, a linebacker." I remembered the lipstick warning. "Justin's actions differed from the kitchen wreckage." Frustration took over. "I don't know. It just bothers me is all."

"You could be right. It wouldn't hurt to remain on your guard."

My head dropped against the pillows. "Speaking of guards, do I still have one, or did your boss get smart?"

His left eyebrow rose. Damn it, even with my regular practicing, I still couldn't do that.

"The guard leaves this afternoon." Dirk paused. "The doctor said you can go home today."

Ginger grabbed her magazines and purse. She jumped from the chair in a move I knew had to have been prearranged.

"You know what? I need something to eat. I'll just run down to the cafeteria for a salad. Can I get you anything?" She asked the question as she reached the door. She looked to Dirk, nodded and waltzed out of the room before I could accuse her of running like Secretariat.

Dirk stepped to my bedside. He placed his thumb against my lips. "Let me have my say before you tell me off, okay?"

My lips curved into a smile. He rubbed his thumb across them then followed up with a brief, deep kiss.

"I know you can take care of yourself, but I worry about you. Nash tried to kill you yesterday. Makes no sense to me because everyone knows you're a church-going preacher's wife type."

I opened my mouth, ready with a smart-ass comeback, but his thumb returned to block my lips.

"Nash may not be the only person who wants you dead."

Shivers ran the length of my spine. Gut reaction? He could be right.

"I want you where I know the territory. If someone else is out there, I can protect you better at my house." His shoulders rose with his inhaled breath. "Stay with me."

I noticed he didn't give me a time limit, just asked me to stay. A little scary, but not anything like what I'd experienced since Morgan died. "Okay."

He closed his mouth. "Okay? That easy?"

I nodded. I hurt and it'd be nice to have someone take care of me. I hadn't had that since my parents died fourteen years ago.

He dropped a quick kiss on my forehead and straightened. "I'll be back to pick you up later. The doctor said he'd release you at three o'clock."

When my brain formed the words, "you don't have to do that," I shut it down. He had a need to pick me up and I wouldn't deny him. Maybe that'd help both of us get past what had almost happened last night. Besides, I had a hunch it'd be awhile before I felt safe in my bungalow.

****

Dirk pushed my wheelchair to the hospital doors himself. The nurse didn't fuss, just handed me off like a pro quarterback passing the ball to his fullback. Not that I cared. They'd given me a shot. I hoped my brain had enough self-preservation cells left to keep me from spouting something stupid. Or worse, mushy. Euww.

He tucked me into the front seat, gave the nurse something to blush about and slid behind the driver's wheel. "Ready?"

"You bet." My hand made a gesture meant to be grand. "Home, Dirk."

He grinned and pulled into traffic, wisely making no comment.

I fell asleep on the short ride and woke up groggy. Dirk threw his arm over my shoulders, holding me to his side. His support kept me from tripping and sprawling at his feet.

His offer of food and drink didn't seem as important as additional sleep, so I staggered down the hall and into his bed. Dirk leaned against the doorjamb, arms crossed over his chest.

"I've got to go to the station for awhile. Can I trust you here or do I have to tie you down?"

I licked my bottom lip and considered his offer. "How about you trust me now and tie me later?"

His dark eyes gave me his nonverbal answer. "A soak will do you good. I'll fire up the spa before I leave because the water takes a couple of hours to heat. Should be ready when I get home."

How had I missed the hot tub? We'd have a hot time in the old tub tonight. My hand covered my yawning mouth. "Sounds great." I'd already rolled onto my side, eyes drooped half shut.

His voice drifted to my ears. "Don't answer the door or go outside until I return."

"'Kay."

Chapter Nineteen

My eyelids flew open. My heart pounded. I didn't know why I'd been jerked awake. Supported on my arms, I listened but everything remained quiet.

Then I heard scuffling outside the window, a ping of pebbles against the glass. I lifted my head. A small boy ducked behind the azalea bushes at the back fence. As I watched, he crouched down and picked up a handful of pebbles.

I slowly rolled out of Dirk's bed, glad I'd remained dressed. My throat ached, and I felt stiff and sore, but I could deal with a small mischief-making boy. I heard more pinging against the window as I left the room. A minute later, I walked onto the deck.

"Hey, stop throwing those pebbles. You could break the window."

No answer. Not even birds chirped. The soft hum of the spa's pump filled the air. "I know you're out here. I saw you hide by the azaleas."

The boy edged out from behind the bushes, but before I could make another move, he darted into the adjoining yard. *Kids.* I made a mental note to tell Dirk he had a potential juvie living next door. Can't turn 'em around too early.

Curious, I moved to the spa for a glimpse of the tub I'd be sharing with Cop Sexy later. I lifted the cover. Sunshine reflected off the water. I winced.

Maybe the pain medication had made me more reckless than usual, but the water's movement hypnotized me. Removing the sectioned Styrofoam cover, I knelt next to the spa.

My gaze caught sight of a sharpened piece of metal lying next to the tub, right under the lip. A garden stake?

I took a closer look, picking up the metal. The stake held pleasant warmth, but I almost dropped it. Darn thing weighed more than I expected. "Basil" had been scrawled at one end. Next to the tub seemed a strange place for safety-conscious Dirk to store a sharp marker, no matter how decorative.

Glancing over the deck, I spotted the reason. A stack of clay pots stood nearby, next to a man-sized bag of potting soil. The tips of other stakes peeked out from a flat of herbs.

Cop Sexy grew his own herbs. He probably had more food in his refrigerator than me too.

The warm metal felt good on my scabbed palm. Plus I couldn't quite pull myself together to move, so I sat contemplating the kind of tough guy who'd grow and label plants. Heck, for all I knew, the stakes and soil were a legacy from his former marriage.

The water's reflection caught my attention again and I reached to test the heat. Warm, chemically treated liquid sloshed over my hand, Nice, but I needed a step above tepid. Even with Cop Sexy by my side the temperature wasn't optimal.

A shadow appeared on the water. At the same time I heard a soft shuffle behind me. Dirk had gotten home earlier than I thought. Crap. He'd be all over me for leaving the house.

The whiff of an expensive scent hit my nostrils. Dirk smelled great, but this odor was perfume, not aftershave. Ginger would have announced herself.

Not Dirk. Not Ginger. Trouble.

Before I could scramble to my feet, a solid push had me sprawled halfway in the water. Crap, not again. Had Justin gotten out on bail?

I flailed. I'm no weakling but the painkiller's effects had left me loopy. If I could get oxygen and a chance, I might survive.

My attacker had determination and a small hand size. A woman, then, not Jason. She didn't let up. I reached behind me to free myself. No dice. I still held the garden stake in my left hand. I turned it face backward. With waning strength, I jabbed up and back.

The attacker's hand let up. Drops of blood landed in the water. I arched my back. Levering my knees against the spa's side, I pushed up and pulled in oxygen. Good thing I did. My still unseen assailant rammed my face back into the water.

The air and reprieve from death fired my blood. My brain cleared. I jabbed the garden stake backward again and again.

More blood floated in the water around me. I didn't let up, just kept my arm moving fast and hard. My vision grayed, my lungs labored. If I hadn't made the high school swim team, I couldn't have withstood the attack.

Pulling strength from despair, I wrapped both hands around the garden stake. I put everything I had into what could be my last defensive move.

The attempt worked.

The hand holding me down slipped away.

I surfaced, gasping for air. I inched my hands up the spa's inner surface, not letting go of the garden stake.

Finally, I pulled free of the water and collapsed next to the spa.

My lungs worked overtime, pulling in oxygen and expelling fear. Luckily, I didn't have to move fast. The would-be murderer lay close by, in worse shape than me.

Bright red hair and thick black glasses were the first items I noticed about the woman. Who the heck was she?

My blurred vision kept me from making an immediate identification. Finally her rock of a wedding ring gave me a clue.

Flash. I'd kept saying she was a criminal but seeing made me a believer.

Slashes from the garden stake decorated her upper body and arms. Blood seeped out of the wounds where she lay sprawled. One part of me hoped I hadn't killed her, another smaller part hoped I had. I might have been shocked at the thought if I weren't so angry. Okay, probably not.

She rolled her head to the side and opened her eyes. "Bitch. Shoulda got you in the cemetery."

My grasp on the stake loosened. Flash had shot at us? "How'd you know we were at Graceland? And why kill us? We didn't do anything to you."

"Followed you." She hauled in a breath. "Took Morgan. Mine. He was…best thing…ever happened."

Revenge. Flash would think and act like a soap opera diva, but murder was too much.

"Has everything. Coulda left him for me."

"Ginger's in love with her husband. She wasn't interested in Morgan."

"Figures." She closed her eyes.

Flash's last words had slurred and she didn't look like she'd be getting up. Still, I held the stake in front of me with two shaking hands. That's how Dirk found us.

He knelt next to me and pulled me into an embrace. His eyes took in the scene. He let go with one hand to phone in a report. That done, he cradled me to him. "I told you not to leave the house."

Surprisingly, his accusation didn't hold much heat.

"The little juvie next door woke me up." I paused to shiver and tried to stop my teeth from chattering.

Dirk pulled a towel from a nearby lounge chair and wrapped it around me. "You mean Johnny? He's not a JD. He's four."

"Don't know his name."

Dirk tightened his hold on me. "He's usually a good kid. He knows not to come over when I'm not home. I wonder what brought him here?"

My shaking had slowed, but a tremor raced through my body. I didn't think it possible, but Dirk held me tighter. Any more clinch and I'd be breathless again.

"I v-v-vote Flash."

The hot sun and Dirk's body heat did their number on my physical shakes. The effects of shock remained, but the major shuddering faded.

I guessed Dirk could tell I'd recovered a bit. "Want to tell me what happened?"

"I'll wait." I only wanted to tell this story once. Or maybe twice, the second time at Flash's trial.

Sirens wailed and grew closer. I eyed him. "Don't you want to change your shirt? Or let go of me before backup arrives? I'm okay with the towel."

"Screw it. I don't care who knows about us. Do you?"

"Not really."

Chapter Twenty

The paramedics bundled Flash onto the gurney and wheeled her off. Meanwhile, the moon-suited techs were back and I'd been shuttled to another part of the yard.

Dirk sat on a lounge chair about five feet away. With him were his neighbor Johnny and Johnny's mother. I rested my head against the chair's back and listened to the little boy's fluting voice.

"Johnny, why don't you tell me what happened, okay? You're not in trouble. We only need to know what you were doing in my yard. Your mom told you not to come over when I'm gone, remember?"

Dirk's soothing voice had me ready to drift off. The rhythmic thuds from Johnny's heels hitting the metal frame slowed and stopped.

"Can you tell us what happened?"

Johnny's chair squeaked. The webbing swished. This I had to see.

The boy crossed both his arms and legs and peeked at Dirk from under his eyelashes. I swanee, all young boys must attend a "get out of trouble with a cute look" class. Looking at Dirk, I realized some of the little monsters never outgrew it.

Johnny uncrossed his arms and rubbed his nose. "The lady with the red hair and glasses gave me a dollar. She said she was Dirk's girlfriend and she wanted to play a trick on him." A big tear ran down his cheek. "But when the door opened, it wasn't you. It was the black haired lady." He stuck out his lower lip. "She yelled at me for being in the yard."

Johnny's mother put her hands on her son's arms. "You know you aren't supposed to talk to strangers." She gave him a little shake. "Or be in this yard without permission."

"But, Mom, the lady said she was Mr. Dirk's friend."

His mother gave a universal mother's frustrated sigh. She raised an apologetic look to Dirk. "I'm sorry, Dirk. He's just so fascinated with you, it's hard to keep him away."

I raised a cynical eyebrow. His mother looked like she shared her son's fascination.

"I'll speak with my husband. We'll figure out how to give you more privacy." She looked my way and winked.

I could have been wrong about the mom.

Johnny plucked at Dirk's wet shirt. "I didn't know she was a bad lady." He ducked his head. "I'm really sorry, Mr. Dirk."

"You ran back home, right? You didn't see anything after the second lady yelled at you?"

I watched Dirk with Johnny. He took care to make sure the kid wouldn't have nightmares about two women in a death struggle. Nice.

"I didn't see nuthin'."

The pressure in my chest relaxed. No kid should have to see violence, not anywhere, real life or television. That was my hot button and I stuck to my opinion. No wonder I didn't want kids.

Exhaustion overtook me. I closed my eyes and let the heat and murmuring voices act as a balm. Young boys, money and dirty tricks. A potent combination. And smart. Her trick had gotten me outside. That still didn't explain Flash's attempts to have me arrested for murder. Or her subsequent attempt to do me in.

The annoying thoughts faded and I slipped into sleep.

****

Dirk and Ginger sat across from me when I struggled to consciousness. I tensed, afraid I'd been transported back to Northeast Medical Center. The dim lighting and comfortable bed convinced me Dirk had kept his promise about keeping me out of the hospital.

Their soft conversation stopped when they noticed me stir. They wore identical expressions of alert worry.

"I'm fine." My raspy voice belied my words, and Ginger offered water.

The room was so quiet I could hear Dirk's phone vibrate. He seemed undecided but answered in a soft voice. He rose and strode out.

My friend clasped my hand. "Katie, I'm sorry I got you involved in my mess. I should have gone to the police when I got that first blackmail note."

"Sweetie, that wouldn't have changed a thing. Once Morgan died, all bets were off."

"But no one should have gotten hurt. Keeping the threats quiet seemed so easy, and I didn't want to be a victim." She paused. "You're so strong, Katie. I thought some of your courage would rub off on me."

I gathered my determination. "You're the brave one, Ginger."

"Me?" She laughed. "Give me a break. You're

never afraid to tell people what you think."

"Sure, but I never tell them how I feel. You do, and that takes real courage." Before I could chicken out, I inhaled a breath and continued. "I love you, Ginger. You're my best friend and I never want to lose you. Ever. I'd do anything to protect you and our friendship."

She didn't bother wiping moisture from her cheeks. "I know. That's why I asked you for help. I knew you'd have my back. In exchange, I almost got you killed."

"Cripes. Give me a break. Flash and I hated each other from the get go. She would've gone after me all on her own."

That was probably true. I had a feeling Flash had thrown me into the mix for two reasons. First, to get back at Ginger for taking Morgan away. Sending Ginger's friend to jail on a murder charge would fit that picture. Second, because we had hate at first look. Or vice versa.

"Ahem." Dirk stood at the door. "Sorry to interrupt but that was the hospital. Brandi Wells will pull through."

The news seemed anticlimactic.

I caught Dirk's alert stance. "Okay."

He frowned. "That's it? That's all you have to say?"

I summoned my new emotional courage. "I know that you will find enough evidence to send her away for years. You'll make sure she goes down for murder and two counts of attempted murder. Or is it three?" I forced myself back on track. "Doesn't matter how many."

I took a deep breath and looked straight at him. "I trust you." I paused. "With my life."

You could have punctured the atmosphere with a

garden stake. Ginger moved away and Dirk took her place at my side, but their moves were nothing more than blurred motion. Tears welled in my eyes and my usual blinking didn't bat them away. Not that I tried hard.

I heard the door click shut but Dirk had already moved to spoon me. He placed his chin on my shoulder. His breath tickled my ear. "Once you make up your mind, you don't waste time, do you?"

"Life's too unpredictable." My parents' death taught me that in middle school and Flash just finished a refresher course.

"I trust you too."

My body relaxed into his. Trust. We had a starting place.

****

Ginger had my back, but I moved pretty well. Considering. We shuffled into the Chocolate Fix arm-in-arm like two old ladies.

Mona slid a tray holding truffles into her glass-fronted sales case. She straightened and began a round of applause picked up by her customers.

Several of the women looked familiar. My feeling was that more than one had been entangled with Morgan. I hadn't killed him, but encouraging the blackmail victims to come forward had saved them all. That act I could get behind without apology.

Ginger guided me to a table, where I eased into a chair. I didn't think we'd be able to stay long. The iron chairs were cute but not so comfy. She walked to the counter and placed our order.

Mona followed Ginger back to the table carrying a plate of truffles and a mug. She set both down with nothing more than a slight click.

"Here you go. On the house."

She pushed the mug closer. "Lemon tea. For your throat."

A sip lubricated my sore pipes. "Thanks."

The older woman waved away my words. "You deserve more than tea, but I'd get busted for serving Champagne without a license."

I couldn't hold back my grin. The mug she'd served me didn't hold lemon tea. Bubbles had tickled the back of my throat when I swallowed.

Around the room, women raised their mugs in silent tribute. I almost couldn't swallow my next sip of "tea." I'd just been in the right place at the wrong time. They'd bared their humiliating stories to the cops. No comparison.

Mona popped a truffle. She chewed, licked her fingers and sipped from her mug. "Have you heard any news on the Flash Front?"

"Dirk told me she heard the Miranda when she came to this morning."

Ginger's mug landed with a clatter. "Did she have a lawyer waiting at her bedside?"

My friend sounded a little testy. "I don't think she had time to call one. She'd better get someone from Charlotte, though. Maybe further out."

"A designer attorney." Ginger snapped her fingers. "I've been meaning to tell you. Remember the lipstick color we tried to match at Nordstrom's?"

"Um, yeah?"

"My cosmetic consultant called this morning. The shade is PowPowRed." Ginger waved her hand. "The shade had limited sales in this area. And guess who bought a tube?"

Mona and I exchanged glances. We answered simultaneously. "Flash."

"You got it." She chose a truffle but couldn't hide a triumphant grin. "Oh, I'm sorry, Mona, you may not know about—"

"The kitchen destruction." Mona nodded. "Yeah, I heard the story. So Flash trashed your house, Katie?"

Ginger swallowed and answered for me. "Yes." She contemplated the plate of chocolates but drank instead.

Mona chose another truffle. "Too bad you can't place her at the scene."

"Au contraire." Ginger gloated, a look I hadn't seen on her face before. "The lipstick is circumstantial, but it fits. I kept the rag I used to wipe down your fridge. Maybe there's DNA."

I figured a charge of B&E and malicious destruction of property was small potatoes compared to murder and attempted murder, but an exercise that'd bring me a world of satisfaction.

Mona saluted Ginger with her mug and drank. "Why'd she use something so distinctive to leave the message?"

"It was last year's shade. She figured no one would recognize the color."

No wonder we hadn't been able to match hues when we went to Nordstroms. The world of the rich. Using a thirty-dollar lipstick to leave a threat.

Ginger frowned. "She began rumors that you'd done the damage yourself. Folks around town know you've got a bit of a temper. No doubt she thought the police wouldn't look further."

Mona jumped in. "She spread stories and pulled strings to make your arrest a sure thing. Sneaky."

She looked at me. "But not as smart as you." She stood. "Gotta get back behind the counter. See me before you leave. The ladies chipped in and bought you a little thank you gift."

****

Ginger used both hands to lift the heavy shopping bag from the Chocolate Fix. The ladies' "little gift" included three boxes of the largest truffle selections Mona sold. They'd also thrown in a small hand painted hat made of solid chocolate. We'd be in sugar overload for weeks. I couldn't wait to open the first box.

Ginger shook her head. "Sick woman."

"Who, me? All I want is to open one of those boxes."

She rolled her eyes. "Not you. Flash."

I crossed my two forefingers in a banish sign. "Don't say that. She could get off on an insanity plea."

"Don't be so sure of that." Dirk and Matt stood at the screen door.

Ginger waved them in. "Would you like tea, Detectives? Cookies?" She gathered mugs and arranged a plate of cookies.

I waited until everyone had settled in then repeated the question. "Why do you think Flash won't get off on an insanity plea?"

"We found traces of ricin in her potting shed. That proves pre-meditation in Anderson's murder. When Nash heard we arrested Brandi Wells for his partner's murder, he turned state's evidence. The DA reviewed the evidence this morning. He's going after her with no plea bargaining."

"So your boss is finally off my back?"

Matt snorted. "Not really."

Dirk smirked. "Are you sure you don't know him?"

"I give up. What's his name?"

"Thomas Fortune."

Ginger gasped. "Tommy? Tubby Tommy is your boss? I don't believe it." She nudged me in the ribs. "You remember Tommy, right?"

"Crap." I buried my face in my hands. Oh, sure, I knew Tommy. I'd stood him up the night of our high school prom. It wouldn't take long for Ginger to remember.

"Katie! Didn't you stand him up on prom night?"

Dirk interrupted before I could answer. "I knew it."

I peeked at him from between my fingers. "Will you be in hot water now that he knows we're dating?"

Matt laughed. "You're kidding, right? Johnson's been in hot water since he started with the force."

Dirk growled in response. He held out his hand to me. "Let's take a walk."

I stood, took his hand and we walked toward Ginger's manicured rose garden. The warm air brought out a medley of aromas created by dozens of rose plants. Bees buzzed and silence lay between us.

"Your job isn't in jeopardy because of me, is it?"

"No."

"Because I don't want to stand in your way or put your career at stake."

"My job's fine."

I exhaled. "Good. That's good."

He put his arm over my shoulders and pulled me against his side. We walked a few more yards, bumping hips occasionally. We stopped under a shade tree and faced each other. He cupped my chin in his palms.

"There's only one thing at stake here." He bent and kissed me. When he pulled away, he said, "Us."

He cleared his throat. "What do you think? Want to take a chance? On me?"

I pulled out my newfound emotional courage to answer him. "Yes, I'll take a chance on you."

He exhaled. "That makes us even then."

I nodded. "Partners."

His lips stopped a hair's breadth from mine. "What do you mean, partners?"

"Well, I knew Flash was bad news from the get go. You wouldn't listen to me. I'd have arrested her right away."

"Without proof?"

I waved my hand and his logic away. "So I figured you could tell me about your cases and I'd tell you what my gut reaction is."

"No way."

"Way."

"I don't have time for this." He captured my lips in a mind-stealing kiss.

I forgot what we'd been talking about, but it didn't matter.

I'd get what I wanted or I wasn't Katie Sheridan.

A word about the author...

Ashantay Peters loves escaping into a well-written book. Her reading addiction also has her perusing magazines, newspapers, Internet articles, and even food labels. The last is often feebly excused as an attempt to maintain health, but her friends know the truth.

She lives in the mountains of western North Carolina, a happy transplant from the much colder (and flatter) Midwest.

Contact the author at www.ashantay.com